LONESOME TWOSOME

LONESOME TWOSOME

Luis Harss

To order additional copies of this book, please contact:
Palibrio
1663 Liberty Drive
Suite 200
Bloomington, IN 47403
Toll Free from the U.S.A 877.407.5847
Toll Free from Mexico 01.800.288.2243
Toll Free from Spain 900.866.949
From other International locations +1.812.671.9757
Fax: 01.812.355.1576
orders@palibrio.com
406773

For who knows for whom nor before whom he speaks.
--MMXII, VII: 22-23--

1

I was looking for Dad. We lived in this trailer park, just outside town, on a slope down to the river. You went in over a speed bump, blop blop. It had a funny name, Waikiki, because the owner was Hawaiian. A moon-faced guy in a flowery shirt. He came by in beach shorts and flip-flops to collect the rent. We were where the dirt road began. They were clearing trees behind us.

Dad wasn't really my dad, but he tried. He took me fishing and we played "punch-you-in-the-nose". He called me Buddy instead of Angie, said I was his girl. Maybe because of my independent spirit, which he thought I'd got from him. One time when Mom threw him out and it happened to be my birthday, which she forgot, he said we were a lonesome twosome. We sat teary-eyed on an oak stump, holding hands. I was gasping because of my asthma. He snorted and thumped me on the back, swore he'd make it up to

me, promised me an army knife I'd been wanting.
He had a paunchy laugh, hair coming out his ears
and neck. A hulking guy with a big shadow. He got
all heated up over his ideas, fighting mad, waving his
arms, but cheery the next moment, slaphappy, he'd
sweep you up into the air, then start bawling again,
when something set him off. Mom wasn't taking any
more of it, she'd cut him loose, she said: "He's gone".
But I knew better. If he wasn't at Rosie's, where I'd
checked and they hadn't seen him, or at his animal
house, which was closed for radon testing, he'd be out
training with the patriots at Camp Liberty. This was a
nowhere place, since it wasn't supposed to exist, out
toward Two Top, behind the cornfields that stretched
way back into the woods. You had to go in deep along
unmarked trails. Everyone knew it was there and that
they practiced military exercises, raids and chases,
but the guys acted as if it was some kind of state
secret. So without a word to anyone, just roaming on
my own, I rode my bike out beyond the factory farm,
to a patch of wild grass where there was a gate across
a ditch. I'd been there a few times, poking around. It
was really just a rotten pole that hung from a chain,
leaning on a fork. It didn't open on to anything but
weeds and brambles. The road out was hot and hazy,
blacktop popping with blisters. It was hard to get that
far anyway, on my crummy old bike with a wobble
and the loose chain that kept slipping off, and short
of breath. And with the crash helmet I had to wear
against brain damage, I could hardly see to find the
gate. But I wheeled on, past snake and deer crossings
and a spot where a groundhog backed into a hole
barking at me.

Round the next curve nothing stirred. Not a breath of air, just the open sky, buzzing bugs in a locust tree gutted by lightning. But then the wild grass swayed along the ditch and a guy came out of the bushes and leaned over the pole gate. Hot and itchy like me, scratching all over. Dressed in sweaty stuff, leopard-spot khakis, combat boots, with a crown of twigs that bristled out on his forehead like antlers, and holding an assault rifle. I knew him: Mac Snack, a dude always loitering at the minimart, by the vending machines, munching chips or pork rinds from a paper bag. Out of work, nothing to do, chatting up the girls, in a net shirt, showing off his tattoos, a dragon and a Grim Reaper. Handy at favors, like rescuing cats from trees or a baby fallen down a well, or letting himself be dunked in a water barrel at the town fair. Maybe a bit of a badass, I'd seen him knock out a man over a bet in a crap shoot. But here he was somebody else, one of those hunters stalking the fields, carrying guns and backpacks, on the lookout for space invaders or whatever. Aliens, they said, smuggled across rivers in inner tubes or dropped from planes by the UN International. They called themselves patriots, went around recruiting people for the home guard. Camping out, singing, saluting, raising the flag. Mac Snack had that look in his eyes. A hot light, like what the Hollerers called soul fire, when the spirit lit them up inside. Acting friends, sort of, he climbed over the ditch: "Hi, Angie". But cradling the rifle and wearing a red armband, which meant beware. They wore all kinds of armbands, black when somebody died, yellow if he went missing, and so on, they all meant something. Anyway, he didn't let me get too close, tiptoeing off my bike. Before I could set a foot on the ground, he stepped forward: "Hey, it's wired". There wasn't even a cow wire that I could see, but I'd heard of an electric fence they'd strung somewhere, with no warning sign, invisible until it zapped you. Shouldering his equipment without letting go of the gun, he kept an eye on me. I asked for Dad and he shrugged and said: "Git along now", and stared past me. But when I didn't move fast enough he suddenly dropped the gun, snatched my bike from under me and twisted it out of shape. I jumped off just in time. He had huge gloved hands that could rip you apart. Cool and easy, he went about bending the bike in several places, turning it into a pile of scrap. I got in some licks, but by then he was done and he plunged back into the bush, sinking out of sight. I heard crackles and snaps, maybe the invisible wire firing off. Then I saw waves moving across the high grass and weeds, like shadows of clouds. You had to go through ragweed and nettles where you'd get shredded. But, beyond, open fields led into the woods and rolling hills. I heard hoots and caws, way out. There were crows as big as buzzards circling overhead, but the noise wasn't coming from them. It was people in the fields making animal calls for signals. Crawling through the underbrush, tearing up trails on dirt bikes, in one of their war games. You could watch them from a knoll wearing horns and antlers and shooting into the air. Some flapped wings like crazy birds, whooping it up.

I was three miles from town and I caught a ride home in a Four By Four that braked for me, honking. This was Jay Bard of JB LANDSCAPING, a farm kid with his own outfit, a tractor mower towed behind and a shovel raised in front, good for all seasons, digging up the roots of trees, dumping snow. My kind of buck, with bulging pockets down the legs of his cargo pants and an earring with a dangling spur, and a sweet guy, not some pimply hayseed popping gum at you, once when I'd asked him to kiss me, just to see what he'd do, he'd said: "We'll need to get your mom's permission for that, Angie". But he'd taught me how to spit through my teeth, like when he squirted tobacco juice, and told me I'd soon look good in a tank top. Going hell-for-leather, plowing into the cars ahead of him, now he came to a screeching stop, the jacked-up truck piling into itself, helped me load the wrecked bike in back with his machinery, hoisted me into the cab, tossing out my helmet, and we took off with a blast, riding high over the tractor-size tires, aiming to sideswipe cars and leaving roadkill.

2

Mom didn't say much, she stuck to her business, in her smock and headscarf, working over the neighbor ladies, who came to have their hair styled, plopped themselves down in a swivel chair that could be cranked up and down, sweaty and fanning themselves, while others sat and rocked on our porch swing, kicking out their legs. She did shags, frizzes, big hair, with foams and spray, washed heads and wigs and blow-dried them. She shaved a lady with a beard, gave a soldier girl a buzz cut. Made them look good in their frumpy dresses, sneakers and white socks, or gauzy fineries, if they were stepping out. Spinning them around while she chatted with her friend Gemma, who worked at the discount store. Gemma was a chainsmoker, with wiry legs, a rasping voice and cough. She'd been a stripper and a cocktail waitress, was learning physical therapy. They took singing lessons together, from the Twins, Gracie and

Angelina, who'd been in show biz. Mom said it was good for her lungs. She had a breathing problem, like me, but it was something else, a gummy feeling in muggy weather, I had to pound her on the chest and back to get her unstuck. She practiced in our outdoor shower and stringing the wash on the line. Gemma had taught her rib cage stretches. And she kept going, never gave Dad a thought. He hadn't been around for a month. He was fading out, like other guys she'd got rid of. He'd never been around that much anyway. Who did he think he was? Just a baggy guy with bow legs who climbed trees with leg and arm grips like a bear, ate in his dump truck, even when he was supposedly at home, still camping out, parked in the gravel by the limestone quarry with the cement mixer that blew dust at us. He came in angry, tramping up the steps, as if straight from a fight, always in a rage over something. Barged in the door and flopped on the couch, flat out, or sat grunting on the can. Dumping his load on the floor like dirty laundry. Army surplus stuff, a bedroll, his mess kit and rations, tin cups. Shoving past us, limping from some old wound and jumping at the sight of his shadow in the mirror, as if somebody was after him, which was what he kept saying, when he packed his guns: "They're out there", there'd been a sighting. Sometimes he groaned in his sleep, woke up out of a big scare, you could tell from his eyes, but he headed out blustering with the guys. He landed on us just to get patched up and fed, Mom said. He battered and shook the house when she wouldn't let him in. Once he came and hitched us to his truck and tried to pull us off our cinder blocks. Then he got out and heaved and almost toppled us, in a rainstorm, splattering waist-deep in the mud.

It was a lifestyle thing with him and the guys. They were firemen, veterans, hardhats from work crews, but also just about anyone you could name, Troy the tackle and gun shop owner, Ace from Ace Hardware, Miller of Miller Meats, Tim Mouse of Heartland Motors, who was in the safety patrol. Always gone, hunting, in and out of season. They gave up everything for it, even Rosie's. They had trackers, weathermen, lookouts in bunkers and tree stands. They dug trenches and moved about disguised in branches. Dad had told me about it, and anyway everyone knew. Sniffers who could scent campfire ashes. A beekeeper wearing his bug suit said he was a minesweeper. Guys on stilts like scarecrows. In high boots, fording rivers. Others in holes or under a net, sprayed with Deep Woods OFF, night-sight goggle eyes like owls, kept watch in the dark. Lying low, then at first light they caught a sound in the breeze, passed it on, a footstep or a voice: "It's them", followed a trail with scat. A person or an animal might run or slip by. They shot at anything that moved, dragged it through the underbrush, and skinned and dressed it right there for cold storage at the factory farm, where they ground it into hamburger. Mom's theory was that they'd gone mad at the animal houses, as she called them, the Elks or Lions or whatever they were, she couldn't tell them apart, but you recognized them when they gathered at fat Rosie's, toasting God's country in the neon haze, baseball caps on backward, or at parades with their flags and marching bands, at the state police stand in the fair, being civic-minded, giving out driver safety brochures. They met in those windowless warehouse-size buildings in clearings or a parking lot off the road, like the Legion post, a spreadeagle on the door. Wrapped in themselves and their body heat, under the whirl of the roof vent or the air conditioner, with piped-in music, filtered so you couldn't tell where it came from, hanging Christmas twinkle lights all year long and air freshener smells. The vent fan vacuuming out the air. We were friends with some cleaning ladies, Merry Maids. They said that in one house the hanging lights floated like spiderwebs. Others had bunting or wind chimes. But everything was very quiet and dim. Even the chimes barely rustled. People came in and stood around. They wore flag pins and medals, stars and stripes. They brought candles and glowsticks. Voices rumbled low when they got going. A lot of new people were joining, swearing allegiance, singing "from sea to shining sea". There were prayers and invocations, witnesses who told of things they'd seen. They'd got religion, Mom said. Like the Hollerers speaking in tongues, even some old guy rolling on the floor when he had a stroke.

There was a house called Temple Lodge. They had a skull and crossbones on the door, like a Poison sign. We knew what went on there because of Becky, who watched from behind a curtain. Girls weren't allowed, but Becky had Down's, which made her special. Besides, her mom was a Word of Life minister. She'd told us Becky was a love child. She looked like a Happy Face button. They were superstitious about her. She'd miss her stop in the school bus and jump off at the Lodge, and they'd let her in and then pretend she wasn't there. Just a ghostly presence, like an angel, people said, though she'd grown boobs and buns, they believed in her. Had her step out sometimes and sing "My Country 'Tis of Thee", in a little dinky voice but with her look of smiley bliss. She spun like a weather vane when she sang, she'd been going to dance school, and she wasn't stupid. If you asked her how she was, she rolled her tongue in her cheek and said: "gifted". She watched everything and told us about it when she came to have her bangs trimmed. Once she'd cut off her pony tail so the kids wouldn't pull it, then changed her mind and had Mom pin it back on like a switch. From what she said, apart from the prayers and songs, they had listening devices, scanners tuned in to the police frequency, the ambulance and the firehouse, so they knew everything that was happening. She showed us how they listened with earphones. She made rabbit ears for an antenna, a zigzag like lightning for a news flash. The gunshop guy was there, the fire marshal and a Rotorooter man who dug septic wells, a "scalper" who skinned animals, the Caterpillar dealer, somebody from homeland security. Big chest-beating guys. Maybe some hardhat girl in a flak jacket, off a bulldozer, or king-sized Queenie, who ran the Valley Motel. They wore their pins, badges and armbands, and lit scented candles that smoked and made you dizzy. The air thinned out and got stuffy. The shadowy hangings felt like sticky tape or flypaper. They went around in circles. The vent fan whirled like a copter rotor above them. It was some kind of magic or mystery. They called it a V-Day. They had their songs and a cheer. A grand master presided. Some wore hoods with eyeslits and a mouth hole. A biker wore a horned owl helmet. They drank from a Halloween skull and burned cross-shaped sparklers that lit up like skeletons. Sometimes a fire sprinkler went off. Or a face shone in the dark. It looked like somebody caught in headlights. There was Skipper, the yellowish black school crossing guard, a freckled albino, and a "legally blind" seeing-eye guy who found lost people for the police. The hunters in camouflage, with their leaves and antlers. Some wore a whole trophy head. They practiced cries and signals. A group did a war whoop. There was a woodsman in a coonskin cap and a Native American with a feather headdress.

Dad's place was a barn with spires. It had its own power source, a monster generator attached to a fuel pump, in case the grid was knocked out. He spent a lot of time there. I could tell when he got back from hunting or his animal house, lumbering like a bear. A black bear had fallen off the tail of a truck going through town, a while back. We'd thought it was an empty pelt, but it turned out to be a live beast that woke from his sleep and rampaged downtown, overturning trash cans, clawing at trees and ripping out parking meters, maybe thinking he heard honeybees inside, because of the way they buzzed when you banged on them. And then a stag somehow got into town hall, went mad butting against the windows trying to get out, and had to be shot, "for his own protection", the cops said, we read it in "The Public Opinion". It reminded me of Dad crashing through the backwoods in camos, bucking and bouncing over ruts in jeeps and ATVs, skinning animals with the scalper, who was also a taxidermist who stuffed and mounted heads that stuck out on his walls as if they'd burst through, one with a huge span, I'd counted twenty one points. In another trailer they had a bear rug and head with open jaws.

3

Things were bad. Guys getting called up all the time, out of their jobs and lives. Soldier girls, too. Off to war somewhere. Some were gone for a year or more. Their kids farmed out to relatives. They'd send a picture postcard from far away, nowhere, "overseas". Maybe a swaggering group photo: "Kicking ass!" Out of place and time. And they came back with that distant look. On a break but still caught out there in their minds. Knocking around for a few days, then back out again. Or they stayed home, but missing that life. Drifting aimless, butting into the furniture. Accustomed to eating and sleeping outdoors. Living from knapsacks, in their trucks. Guns slung across the back seat rack. Kids copied them, pissing into the open, blowing snots through their fingers. They gathered at rallies and tailgate parties with kegs and boomboxes, or on a sweet-smoking high. Crazy guys, hooked on that other life. A lot of them sick or wounded, but still fighting out there, "worldwide", they said in talk radio, and on the home front, too. Like Andy Penn and his girl, Mary Mountain, in the "boater" down the lane. They used to work in the carwash at the Sun service station. In wetsuits, like surfers, splashing soapy suds on the kids who ran through. Now they rammed up and down the road, hunting for intruders. Part of a quick reaction team, "minute men". They'd been in a round-up, put some stragglers across the state line. Sometimes they just rolled over them, hit and run. They chased curtained camper vans. You heard all sorts of stories. Sightings in dumps and drainage pipes, miles of tunnels dug by hand, a corn maze that had been broken through, a burned patch in a field that was a secret landing pad, a road with tar drippings that looked like some kind of writing with a hidden message. I knew of paths where spiderwebs formed so fast that you couldn't tell anyone had been by. A tramp at the old water mill had once groped me. They tracked people for days, let them move ahead and lead them to others. Caught them and left them tied up in a barn. Beat them out of bushes. People scattered, lost, wandering along the road, who turned themselves in without a fight. Maybe just field hands, gypsy workers, but it could have been a suicide bomber headed for the dam or the power plant. And others got by, a lot of them, or maybe just a few, but you kept running into them. They were already in town, at low-wage jobs, in fast food joints or at construction sites, shacking up in flophouses or the Sigmar Hotel, which had a sleazy sweatshop in the basement. We'd heard of families living in boxcars in the railyards. Others went by in battered cars with clanging tailpipes. A tractor trailer had overturned on a bridge, half-smothered people spilling out of the container. Cheap labor that stole jobs from us, the guys said, or welfare bums.

They talked about it at Rosie's. Drinking to bust their belts and arm-wrestling, working themselves up into a fury. Playing the juke, throwing darts at a corkboard woman who stuck a fat butt out at them. Rosie was like her, a big mama type, but with a butch haircut. She belted out songs with them. Truckers and bikers came, heavy metal gleaming. Sat and stewed in the buzz and glow of the neon beer ads. They fed the juke, which shot out light rays. Silent brooding loners and loudmouths. Hunters and nightriders. I went with Mom to listen to the music. There was also karaoke once a week, they turned on a sound system. A spacey bargirl wore rings in her ears, nose and lips, and where else? She played in a punk band downtown. Mort Damon, a guy with a rental car business, dropped us off or we'd go walking along the highway. They let me sit at the bar with Mom. I sipped a soda through a long straw that bent at an elbow. Gemma came by after work, tired out from struggling with sprains and backaches. A crick in her neck, too, and a sour breath. She said it was a worry breath. We'd pick up news and talk. Mom with her throaty voice, like a torch singer. She had a way with the guys, knew how to listen and make them laugh. Gemma hanging tough, joked and blew smoke at them. Soon they'd be up dancing. The guys horning in on each other. I'd get a turn, standing on some guy's shoes. A trucker would know a road song. Mom would join in and remember it afterwards. Days or weeks later, it would come back to her. Word of the war and the world went around. Three TV screens on brackets over the chrome bar showed all-state ball games, championship wrestling. There were pictures of Hall of Fame heroes on the walls, trophy cups on shelves. A floor fan blew paper streamers. You sat in a cool shade, a breeze coming your way. Just hanging out, passing time. The karaoke machine making sound waves. Heads in an electric haze around you. Heated guys chilling, leaving streaks in the air when they gestured. They drank and played pool and poker in a back room. Loud and edgy, trying to unwind, but venting their hates and hang-ups. Always somebody with war wounds or cut up in a work accident. A hunk of a guy, big as a ten-ton truck, choking up over a lost buddy. They unloaded on Mom, who hugged them, pulled a head out of a puddle of beer. I got to hear things, too, because of the mask I wore on dusty days, like a muzzle, they said it meant I could keep a secret. But you just had to look around. Lives breaking up, lost homes and jobs. We'd seen neighbors being evicted. A family we knew, holed up in their rundown trailer. Like survivalists, with all their earthly belongings, dug in and armed. The guy had been laid off while he was away, though they were supposed to have saved his job for him, cleaned out, he swore he'd kill himself. He'd been firing warning shots every time someone came near. He had a "take-home" wife, from one of those wars overseas, a baby doll type with slant eyes, and her mama or granny, a screechy old hag. The Hawaiian got them to come out with some trick. They had a fish tank, shot full of holes, draining fast, writhing fish all over the place. They bundled their kids out, carrying the mama or granny in a sling. The Hawaiian went around checking on people, hustling out deadbeats with his barrelchested bodyguard and bouncer, Lamar. They banged on doors or just broke in, strong-armed people into their cars and over the speed bump, pointed downhill, if their gas tank was empty. Some fought back, but most had already been hit so hard they just gave up.

In another trailer there was a strange yard sale, in the evening instead of the morning. Out by the water pump, in the late summer light. A big flabby family laying things out on folding tables. The lady in a shift, girls in clogs, blobby kids of all sizes dropping things. They were noisy, sloppy army people, the kids in rags, diapers and undies strung up everywhere, toys left out in the dirt, kickballs, a bigwheel. They'd moved in just months before, lugging duffel bags and a boombox. Based nearby at Fort Starr, waiting for housing, they said. They'd patched up the place, scrounged around for pans and basic furniture, settled in on fleabag mattresses. A torn porch screen, rubble on the roof, dried-up ivy peeling off the siding, everything falling apart, a fender-bender-shaped underskirt, plants in cracked pots, and the boombox pounding, almost knocked you over when you went by. Needy, beat-up people. A damp breath blew out the door, with a stale kitchen smell. Chickens scratched in the weedy yard, a mangy dog flopped on their doormat. The guy came and went from barracks, in and out of uniform, killed time working around the house, in dirty work clothes, leaving his fingermarks on the walls. A busy, bustling guy. Nobody understood his name. His kids and his lady called him Papi. Only Mom could speak to him, in that way she had. She said he reminded her of someone she used to know, and once I saw her laughing with him. But now he hadn't been seen for a while, there was just his lady, sprawled out, the kids all over her, a baby dangling from a tit she didn't bother to flip back in all the way between feedings. She'd tried having a day care but there already was a Mama Bear Day Care, and she couldn't borrow any more time or money for the rent, so they were selling out. They'd set out kitchen and yard stuff, a lot more than you would have thought they'd have, considering the short time they'd lived there, grimy pans, mason jars, a barbecue grill. And frills, flowervases, lace doilies, pretty things you wouldn't have expected, a sunflower-shaped wall clock with a calendar. People came by to nose around. Invited themselves in as if they owned the place. Jack Bargain, the hard luck man, was there, looking things over. I went with Mom, who needed shoe pockets. We found a rack with empty clothesbags on wire hangers, stiff as mummies. There was a moldy refrigerator, mushy carpets, a sunken davenport, a junky TV spluttered on and off, all in a blur of sound, the boombox on so loud you almost stopped hearing it, only felt the throb. We looked for the lady, who used to come over for a free hair-do, the only thing in the world that cheered her up, but the kids shooed us out. It was late, getting dark. The sale went on by lamplight. More people stopping by, mostly fingering items without buying. But the family began giving the things away, handing them to anyone who picked one up. People helped themselves, others stood around or sat on stools and camp chairs. Sort of landing and sinking in. Drawn to the place, some out of bed, in nightclothes. Aching backs, still half asleep. Guys with six-packs stretching their legs out. A moment before, they'd been pitching horseshoes out back, the kids rollicking around. But now everyone just sat there bugeyed in the shadowy light and night smells, cooking smokes and garbage, you couldn't breathe. Flitting moths got caught in your hair. The sky like a dark awning over us. The kitchen and yard stuff was all gone. A few knickknacks were left, a picture frame standing without a picture, just a framed hole, lit from the inside by a candle lightbulb, a little glass flame on a stem, like the ones people put in windows. The moths fluttered into it and burned up as if the flame was real. Jack Bargain was still there, picking at things. Some Hollerers came by to mourn. It was like a wake, only without a body. But when the candle bulb went out, Mom said she saw a head hanging in the hole of the picture frame.

4

Then one day Dad came for me. On an urge, as usual, when he happened to think of me, he drove up raising a storm, ditched the truck, jumping out in baggy khakis: "Where's my Buddy?" Bandy-legged and with aching bones from the hardships of life in the bush. Back to take me fishing in the river, like old times. "Just me and my girl, how about it?" We had to prepare for it. Cozying up to Mom, wheedling and pleading, he got permission to spend the night. She let him sleep in his bedroll on the porch. He tossed around with his bad dreams, got me up with a flashlight to dig for nightcrawlers. He had a net and tackle with him, flies hooked in his fishing vest, power bait, they were part of his camping gear, like his beer cooler. What he didn't have he made on the spot. He whittled bamboo rods, strung corks as bobs on a line, split shot on another line to sink it. A know-how can-do guy with the fifteen-blade pocket knife he'd been meaning to give me. Jittery but happy with me. We slipped and slid down the embankment. I took a pail and wore hip-high boots, my hooks in a cartridge belt.

It was a great river day. People sunning and boating, ducks paddling by, kids swinging from ropes out over the water in clouds of gnats. He knew all sorts of wilderness adventure type things, like how to follow undercurrents. We waded in and upstream, a quarter of a mile, away from town, past the stink of drains and sewers, a waterfront warehouse. It was sludgy, hard going. Tangles of driftwood swirled in eddies. We broke through, fought the pull. Backing forward, trailing our lines. He dragged me along with his angry force. We ran into a pack of kids from the shacks. They were jack-jumping in life preservers off a flatbottom boat that knocked against a rotten pier. Bums bathed and did mouthwashes, crumbling when they dried out on the bank. They'd hung scabby rags with sleeves and legs from a wire fence. One was fishing for fingerlings with a net that had a hole in it. Another sifted dirt in a pan. We looked for weed beds, shallows below riffles and fallen trees where bass lurked. We caught a catfish like an old shoe, except for the whiskers. A bullhead, but smart as hell, Dad said, it could walk on its tail as well as swim, and knew its way, so that if a river dried up it moved to another one, he'd seen it crossing the road at a traffic light! He was full of such stories: a puffer he'd once pulled out, bloated up and blowing foam like bubblegum. Another time it was a toadfish with baggy jowls, panting, a bottom feeder. Now we were expecting en electric eel, meaning a snake. He used to fly a "Don't tread on me" flag with a picture of a coiled snake. We were almost chest-deep, at least I was, in midstream. Like Hollerers getting baptized, going under and back out, born again. A buzz of bugs around us, overhanging branches flicking in our faces. He swatted and flayed the air, lost his footing, came crashing down, got up with a big splash. We'd shed half our things, but we kept going, hellbent. We were looking for a trout brook fed by a cold spring, where the water ran clear over a rocky bottom. Farther out, past the reservoir. Instead we got into swampy water with side pools. Water plants with floating bladders clung to us, suckers and web feet. Dad said people could lie low and hide in the elder bushes, breathing through reeds. A while back we'd seen a gaping mouth and eyes watching us from under the roots of a tree. We waved off dragonflies, flying beetles, big as roaches, and whirly bugs with propellers. We cast a line with a lure and felt a bite, probably the electric eel, because it gave me a shock. We played it but it got away, before we could reel it in, and so did a flashy silvertail, maybe a pike, or just some spiny panfish, taking his hook, line and sinker with it. By then he was fed up, he said it was easier to shoot them out of the water, like they did at camp. The same with the bugs, you had to wipe them out: "It's them or us". He seemed to have flipped. Thrashing and wheeling around, as we headed back, he kept shouting: "They're taking over". I thought of the people hiding in the rushes, swimming underwater. He said if we waited long enough we'd see one go floating by.

We got home wet and muddy. Weeds hanging from us like wilted lettuce. It was late and he had a chill and Mom felt sorry for him, shivering there, eating his grub from a can, and let him stay the night again out on the porch.

5

He left a mess. He'd had the guys over with a keg. But we picked up and moved on. Mom with some big hair days. Goddess styles for wedding pictures, close crops for fighting girls. And she had her singing lessons with Gracie and Angelina, who said she was a natural, just needed practice. They plunked out songs on a tinny piano with noisy pedals, in their park model Roadrunner, which they called the bandwagon. Toothy ladies with golden locks. They used to be The Singing Twins in carnivals and elections. They'd been on radio and TV, had a Music Row agent, almost made the Top Ten. Now they'd been born again, which was sort of like making a comeback, they sang gospel at the auction house. And they still knew their rock, blues, country-and-western. Once a week they sang at the Cowboy Saloon. This was the roadhouse on the strip with a buffalo head over the door, a patriot hangout. They were hiring singing waitresses, babes and cowgirls. Mom and Gemma went to try out, just for kicks, though Gemma couldn't hold a note in a bucket. They drove out in her old clunker, which looked like it had been in a demolition derby. Gussied up, Mom in skinny jeans, Gemma in hot pants. Talking as if they were in a musical, singing their lines. They'd rehearsed with a little electric keyboard we had in a case. Mom could play a few chords on it to get started. It was the happy hour, with a drink on the house, so there was an audience. The band played oldtime favorites, lots of fiddles and harmonicas. Yodeling yokels sounded like auctioneers. There was a box stage with a spotlight. The ladies spun ropes, a pistol-packing mamma twiddled a six-shooter. Some of it went over and some didn't. Mom made twangy sounds which set the mike off on its own. Guys hassling her, cracking up over their own jokes. Gemma did a saddle song with giddyaps.

Then there was karaoke night at Rosie's. People waving and yelling, hip-swinging, hard-hitting stuff, with music video effects. Gemma sang "Ruby Lips", blowing heart-shaped kisses. Wound round the mike as if it was a streetlamp, in a see-through wrap of neon light she slithered out of like a skin, doing a bump and grind. A broad with a spread. Mom sang one or two things that were going around, she'd been working on them. Then a song only she knew, which came to her sometimes. In her throaty voice, with a hollowed-out look. Gone somewhere, way back, she'd hear it in her head, suddenly, feel it in her throat. So deep down and hush hush it was barely a whisper, almost just her lips moving. Her own song, she'd told me, with her own words. For just a moment, it would come and go. Blow off and on again, like a party candle. Everyone gaping at her, like: "Come out of it!" But she had a hit with Gemma, a patriot song, "Skyriders", from a movie about astronauts, even the heavy metal guys loved it. She also sang with the Hollerers, who had an open mike. We weren't real believers, but she liked the music, "rock and rise". They went around in their Faith Van, a billboard truck that used to advertise an America The Beautiful theme park. They'd started in a store front, sitting on up-ended crates, now they had a revival tent with Old Glory stripes on Half Mile Island, which they'd turned into a parking lot, and a boat-shaped shrine they called the Salvation Ark, with hot ticket shows. The pastor, Doctor Joy, was from Almost Heaven, it was on his license plate. He'd been an addict-- a dentist on happy gas-- but seen the Lord, at a Lion's Den adult superstore, Gemma said. They baptized people in the river, dunked them in tunics and put a Born Again sticker on their foreheads. They rolled down an astroturf aisle during worship, chanting and witnessing, spun prayer wheels like pinwheels. They healed broken bones and wounds, painful memories, any kind of ache or suffering, somebody who cried and couldn't stop, a fat lady on a diet, starving herself but didn't lose weight. The pastor told her she was fat with grief. A paralytic propped up for him he cured with a pushover. Landed him flat on his back and made him get up, told him to walk on water, and gave him a spirit level to keep his balance. And all the time there was the choir, everyone chiming in, even babies holding hymn cards. They sang about Heaven being "wild and wonderful". Some big brassy voice leading, but anyone could stand up and sing solo, if the Spirit moved him, and when Mom tried it they said she was blessed.

6

I went to school. First I'd been with some home
schoolers. Mom wanted me near her. We'd just
arrived and weren't planning to stick around. A long
distance trucker had dropped us off. A man without
a home, except for the rented trailer where he'd left
us. It had a cot and the porch swing. We didn't know
anyone, but the home schoolers came by. They'd set
themselves up in a shack-style trailer with a leaky
air-conditioner, hot as a boiler room. They said they
didn't trust the system. A Milky Way Dairy girl in a
bonnet taught us, with Bible pictures. She said we
were descended from angels, not monkeys, as godless
people claimed, except maybe some of the kids from
the camper vans. We felt our shoulderblades for knobs
of wings. The air-conditioner made noise without
air. Linty fabric softener floated in through a broken
window. There was a laundromat nextdoor. Then,
the way things went, as the trucker never returned

and we stayed on, Mom having developed other attachments, I'd moved to the real school, an old redbrick ruin they were using while they built a new school with a sports dome. They bussed us out, even those who lived close enough to walk, put us through security checks, patdowns, beepers. SAFETY FIRST signs, NO GUNS. Jock types pushing you around, slamming you into lockers as they went by. The toilets backed-up, gangs marking turf with gobs of spit. Rollerbladers and glue-sniffers, freaky hoops players, eight feet tall. A lot of beefy kids, tugging at themselves, let you know who was boss. "Gunning" for you. Bully girls, too, showing rank, blowing gum in your face. Preacher kids ranted and speechified. Spreading the Word. We had emergency drills. Evacuations in battle formation. Coaches took us on hikes up freedom trails, carrying daypacks. There were Explorer scouts and army brats.

We'd had a cold snap. The trees were changing colors. A forest ranger from the state park taught us survival skills. In case of total war, he said. We dug for water, made fire rubbing stones and twigs, ate berries and roots, loaded a shotgun. Blending into our surroundings, which was easy, with the leaves piling up around us. We kept on after school, had hideouts in woodpiles and tool sheds, practiced rolling down a slope, chewing dirt. Lying low all day to jump an enemy. Falling into a pool of shit in an outhouse. A kid with guns at home said he was going to smuggle them in and shoot up the school, he had a floor map. There was a jock girl who wrestled guys down with a broken arm in a cast. Her mom was a drill sergeant, barked out boot camp orders in phys ed. Then there

were the special kids like Becky. It meant they had
some weird gift or power—an amazing grace, Becky
said. They ran in a special olympic, their art work
was hung in the halls. Becky was a mascot at ball
games. The pom-pom squad carried her out in a letter
sweater, twirling a baton, they said she spooked the
other team.

I also knew my way around. Following my Lone
Star. Mean as the next guy. I had a chipped tooth,
climbed trees, could throw a punch or kick some jerk
where it hurt, I didn't even have to aim. Pals with
Frisbee, a black boy with dreadlocks, darker than his
shadow but with an evil gleam. We'd had child labor
jobs together at the packing plant and the cheese
house. We did raps and a hip hop, sharing earbuds.
It meant the Force was with us. He'd seen my dark
side, said it was a birthmark. I'd wear my dust mask
or sniff my asthma inhalant. Once, stirring melted
cheese in a hot vat, I'd swelled up with an allergy.

Everyone knew some trick. A backwoods kid
played dead when he was attacked, he even stank,
as if his corpse was rotting. Another kid had a metal
plate on the back of his head, said it caught radio
messages. Another joined live wires with his bare
hands. They flashed blades, a magnifying glass that
shot death rays. A patriot kid could stand pain, torture,
arm twists, you couldn't get a squeak out of him. Just
in case, he carried a suicide pill under his tongue,
ready to pop. A lot of strange kids, some from the
camper vans, the gypsy workers who were moving
in, jobbers at various projects. Pudgy guys with
wispy beards, breasty women brimming over. Cheap
housing was going up for them, tenements. So many

of them that they worked and slept in shifts. Come and gone overnight, the kids, too, kept to themselves, wouldn't even give their names in class. They ganged up in corners, speaking their language. But they were friendly with me. I didn't mind being around them. They'd given me the once-over. And they could talk American dirty talk. One kid offered me his chili dog. He'd figured out how to say that. And they had some dreamy girls, with kinky curls or long thick braids. They'd all been to the hairdresser. They wore charms and glittery pictures of saints. One girl in my grade was pregnant. She couldn't hide her baby bump. She had patches of white skin, like scars from burns. She talked to me as if I understood. She let me listen to the baby. It made whooshing sounds, not at all like her shrill voice. She called it Jesus, which was one of their names, but pronounced different. Like when they said "holy", it sounded like "holly". It freaked out some preacher kids, smarty pants from a Bible science class, who were wising up the gypsy kids, teaching them intelligent design, which was about the world not being as old as ignorant people thought it was and the dinosaurs still being alive, they'd seen one in the quarry, which had been closed off when a drunk drowned in a swimming hole, so you couldn't go. But in one of the new modular homes along roadside strips of farmland, with solar panels, they were raising an ostrich in a pen, and it flapped stubby wings and laid huge prehistoric-looking eggs in a nest in the ground.

7

Mom had a new guy, big Joe Marvel, who drove a creamy white Cadillac, once an airport limo, knew all the shortcuts, he took us in cushy comfort to the mall. But I still thought of Dad. I went out looking for him again. Jay Bard had untangled and oiled my bike and put in five speeds to get me up hills. I chased some buzzard-size crows down the road. They thumped on their crops and batted wings against the pavement to take off.

It was a breezy, hay-feverish day. Gnats and dandelion wheels flitted into my face. I had to gasp for air to blow them away. I was also twisting in my skin. Suddenly burning up, my joints sore. Growing pains, Mom said. It felt like hot hands all over me, inside the gym clothes I'd worn for protection. I heard shots everywhere, even in the nearby fields, the put-puts echoing in the hills, it was hunting season. Stalkers on the loose. Even half-baked kids playing big shots.

I'd heard of being hit by "friendly fire". I ditched my bike and ducked into the bushes, at another entry point I knew for Camp Liberty, over a cattle guard. A spot with no gate, just spikes and brambles clawing at you, then a potholed trail. Maybe one of those Indian footpaths that used to criscross the country, Dad had told me, rights of way in what used to be their happy hunting grounds where their spirits still went by, so I was on to something. Following my Lone Star, which was like the global positioning satellite beacon some guys said they connected their trucks to. Torn ragged by the sawgrass, I made my way, watching for signs, expecting to be caught in a trap, a stake driven through my heart, or strung by a foot from a tree. I knew there were patrols, not too far away, I heard their yawps and calls. Bushwhackers scaring out the lead-bellied crows that flapped up, windblown, like black kites. I imagined them on long strings, hovering up there, part of an early warning system. Soon I was picked up by some guys who stormed by in a muscle car, armored like a humvee but open on top, waving guns, dangling legs over the sides. No sign of Dad, but Mac Snack, riding backward, reached out and yanked me on board, laughing when I slugged him: "Hop in, hottie!" And they tossed me around on laps and shoulders, a bunch of roughnecks I knew, bouncing along a hard-scrabble trail, over clods of earth with dry roots sticking out like bones. They had cell phones and walkie-talkies. A guy with a headphone intercepted signals. He let me listen to different wavelengths, tuning in, losing them and picking them up again, a buzz of live wires in the air. There were high-pitched whistles: "Brain waves", he said, it meant aliens close-by. Blots of figures they were tracking, running them down, flushing them out: "Dead or alive!" We'd painted shark teeth on our fenders, a killer smile. All the gun-toting swashbucklers around town, trigger-happy Hal from True Value, who used doves and squirrels for target practice, King Burger of the factory farm, a print shop guy who said he had a 3-D printer that made guns, coach Rocky "Rambo", who bred fighting dogs, shot them when they lost. Eight, ten men in all, Skipper the black albino, the "legally blind" seeing-eye who was psychic, a bomb squad man who rode out front with a metal detector that was also a minesweeper. We met other patrols, loose guns and special forces with birdwatchers, waterfinders with forked sticks, deadshots with scopes, field glasses, cool-hand gun club marksmen, stalkers who could read tracks, rustling leaves, a flight of squawking birds. The whole place seemed wired. You could sense when "they" were around. Sensors went off like guns: "Yonder!" Screeches and pings, and the heavies took over, swept down on a fallen tree with a rag caught in the branches. I was right in there with them, a hawk-eyed scout. Wind-whipped, flying out ahead. Trucks with tarps and pirate flags went by in blurs of dust. I saw barbed wire barriers, POSTED signs everywhere, trenches, trap holes, a hoodie jacket dangling from a noose. We crossed a NO HUNTING area with a game warden. Woods and remains of crops plowed back into the ground and fields of haystacks, plastic wraps ballooning in the wind, held down with tires, tattered scarecrow crosses with stuffed arms and legs.

A rocky trail led through chopped corn stalks, all the way to the hills. Mountaineers kept watch there, guides and lookouts, part of the home guard. And some who'd gone over to the other side, I'd heard, hid illegals in their shacks and woodsheds up dead-end roads. We ran into a snake man, dressed in skins, with a goiter, he came out of a dugout, where he kept his shaggy old lady and kids, holding a snake by the jaws with pincer fingers, which was how he milked it of the poison he sold for antidotes, he gave us directions up a back way. I kept seeing things, or thought I did. Moving bushes, shapes of people making ripples in the grass. The guys bugeyed in the dimming light. Some with the hot eyes of Hollerers. A sort of blind faith or vision driving us. Scanning space from a ridge. The sun flaming out along the skyline. We crossed an open patch of scorched earth. A guy who knew about flying saucers said it was a landing pad. Maybe space invaders, or a UN chopper or the Feds. Becky said they were like action figures, but life-size. And meantime those pop-up beings wandering around, watching us as we watched for them, I had that feeling. A guy let me take a shot at a shadow. I couldn't tell if I'd hit anything, it was getting dark, night closing in. The guys with wild manes, biker whiskers and beards, headscarfs knotted behind their ears. We followed a hard trail, dry as a snakeskin. Lit our way with headlights, spotlights on the trees. We pulled over and listened, the motor and lights out. Using a still-hunting technique. Guys with goggles, trying to see. One had natural night vision. He drove when we took off again in the dark. A black man shouting: "Woe! Woe!" We came out on a larger group gathered round a bonfire. Happened to be a campsite I knew, it used to be the scouts' Camp Jamboree. By a stream, now dried up. But the stakes of tents still stuck out. Muscle cars and off-roaders parked all around. They'd run up the flag and were working at keeping the fire going, threw whole bushes into it, which a guy lit by shooting a flame at them with a blowtorch, if they didn't catch on right away. I saw a lot of animal house faces. It was one of their V-Days. They wore their branches and camos, all crusted over. Jungle pants and quilted vests. Man-up makeover on some man-size girls, warpaint, blackened teeth. Gum-chewing, tobacco-spurting all-weather guys leaning into the fire, with overgrown foreheads and backs. Battle weary or plain drop-dead tired after some long trek, they spat and grilled hamburgers, downed hip pocket drinks that tore them up inside. We unloaded with them, packs and flap pockets. Ate and guzzled, washed and booted up again. An all-star team, guns pointed everywhichway. The fire snapping and throwing sparks. We stoked it late into the night. The eyes of beasts watched us. Meaning the enemy who was out there, I could tell, whenever a guy jumped up and listened, maybe did a round along the edge of the light, others backing up against each other or huddled into themselves, plugs of Mail Pouch in their cheeks like a toothache. Shadowy presences reached for us, you felt the pull, like a sudden choke hold. I kept catching a high-pitched whistle close-by. It was a guy with a hearing aid. Another croaked like a frog through a speaker in his throat. The guy with the hearing aid let me try it. It was dirty with earwax, but the moment I plugged it in I heard rustlings in the bush, whispery steps, just the sounds I'd imagined would come from the pale figures you saw through night vision goggles, it made your skin crawl. Some guys had the shakes. I heard loud chattering teeth. Bodies piled up, mounds of flesh, couples in bedrolls, making out like mad, guys unwinding bandages. They sang under their breaths, holding hands all together in a power grip. A cold drizzle soaked us through. Our clothes shrank on us. A patrol still went around wearing canvas sacks like cloaks. Guys with night sight but good as blind, shooting into the dark. We burned a scarecrow cross. It jumped and waved like a drunk in a barn dance. A hand gripped me: "You show, girl!" It was Mac Snack giving me a boost. He'd already let me take a swig from his flask. I bummed a cigarette from somebody else. Then a kind of glittter sprinkled us, from a clear sky, probably radioactive fallout. They said there was a secret nuclear waste dump in Bald Mountain, where your hair fell off, and the gleam of fluoride in the reservoir.

A noisy truck took me back to town, a wrecker with whirling lights and blinkers and a loud beep. We ran out of gas, barely made it, but I kept going the next day. Coasting along with Jay Bard and his partner Chad, who was teaching me how to shoot with his .22 squirrel gun. They picked me up off the school bus when it broke down at the railway crossing. Carried me around all day with their machinery. They were landscaping the Midtown Bank, planting, digging things up. Flower boxes, carved shrubs, spindly trees in mulch, they had a master plan, year round. We went on to Terrace Apartments out by the

airport, where Mom used to clean rental properties
before she had the beauty business. I helped them
roll up the lawn, run branches through a grinder that
made sawdust. At Fountainhead, a picture perfect
neighborhood, we trimmed bushes, knockout roses.
They had a temple-shaped greenhouse. We ate at a
drive-in, snuggling and steaming up, lifelong buddies,
in good and bad times, we split a jumbo sub and fries
three ways, drank from the same straw. Then riding
high and mighty, out on the road, we passed a kiss
along, with a gob of spit. Chad drove, veering wildly.
A jerky kid, with quick-fire impulses, and mad about
me, he'd taken me on a drag race up the mileground,
an old airport runway. We practiced my shooting in
the gravel pit, scaring up the buzzard crows, which
sometimes swept down clawing the air and vomited
on you. Anything I wanted, out for thrills in his
stripped-down racer, hydroplaning, jumping ditches
or skirting a roadblock, chasing a hedgehopper across
a field, I couldn't get enough.

8

Meantime I took care of Mom. She'd broken with Joe Marvel. Suddenly panicky, it happened to her every time, she'd woken up one day, seen him there yawning and scratching his armpits: "Who's this guy?" She remembered what really mattered: "It's just you and me, Angie, hear?" Then Dad had called with threats. Nothing to do with Joe Marvel, just one of his binges. I heard him shouting and swearing over the phone. We'd had it reconnected after months of not paying the bill, because of a long distance call Mom was expecting, after one of her out-of-body experiences, from a mysterious agent she called an angel. But it was Dad each time. She said he sounded wayward, meaning he was loose somewhere, like when he groaned in his sleep and woke up from a bad dream saying they were after him. She'd hang up on him, or the line went dead, but he called again, just breathing on us. As if he was standing right outside the door. It was scary, once the customers were gone, out in our corner of empty lots with bare trees you could see through.

Shut up in our tin can, behind closed blinds, we had to get out and breathe. So we went neighboring, down the dirt path to the main area with paved alleys. A wet wind blew us along, leaves splattered us. There was a dingy autumn light, the world seemed used up, maybe about to be snowed in, but everyone was out splurging energies, doing house repairs, junking appliances down the slope. Heavy-duty guys with power tools drilling, pulling to start motors, leaf blowers, whatever, throwing themselves into it, climbing a metal staircase up the water tank, running illegal power cables, a guy on a roof branching out an antenna mast, a wingspread into the sky, didn't care if he fell off and broke his neck. Cars rattled in from work. Rovers and off-roaders back from patrol. Hotrodders picked up babes in souped-up Mustangs and Camaros. Life carrying on bigtime, fights, parties, cookouts. We went around taking in the news. Guys hurt or missing, a fundraiser for the family, maybe an animal house barbecue, a rally somewhere, an all-night watch that drew folks in like sleepwalkers. Or stir-crazy people making noise, shooting hoops, pumping iron, kids bouncing on a trampoline, toys scattered about and other stuff, sandboxes, birdfeeders, kiddie pools, hanging plants, cat litter. Flags on flagpoles, spreadeagles on doors. We bumped into some old guy who carved decoys. A home shop sold toy bears that were like stuffed pets. There was a tattoo artist. He'd offered me a "Come and get me" tattoo. Everyone doing his thing,

polishing a gun barrel, ripping the guts out of a car.
The lights of the WAIKIKI office signboard buzzed
with bugs. A loudspeaker played electric ukulele
music. When it was off it made white noise like fuzz.
Sometimes Gemma came along, on a whistle-stop
tour, her flame-red hair turning pink in the blaze of a
neon sign. She did "sick calls", practicing her therapy
on aching joints, cramps, slipped discs, anything she
got her hands on, some pukey guy with the bends,
just so she could slap him around, Mom said. We
dropped in on the Twins or a yard sale. A dressmaker
made woman-size dresses. She called herself Dora
Belle. There was Jack's Bargains, with all the junk
he'd bought up. In good weather it spread out like
a fleamarket. A lot of busy business. Garbage fires
burned in oil drums. We breathed it all in, rising river
smells, smoke from the dump in a mound behind the
trees, with gulls circling overhead, so far from the
sea, something must have smelled fishy to them, I
could taste it on my skin. We stopped at an eatery in a
trailer window for a Kool Aid or a juice box. A shot of
moonshine for Gemma, from some backyard brewery.
Another home-brew place, where there'd been a
drug bust, was cut off by a yellow crime tape. One
time we crashed a wedding party. A big blonde and
her guy, both fighters, in camos. Everyone boozing
up, taking flash photos. There was an emcee on a
wireless mike, a DJ with earphones. Kids and oldies
piled in. They drank sparkling cider and hard stuff.
A fatty called Butterball sang an uplifting song. The
weddies held balloons, His and Hers. They surfed the
crowd, over a mosh pit, and were off to the front in
the honeymoon car, trailing Bud cans on strings. Wild

rock pounded and wailed. Down the lane a boobsy girl nursed several babies. Hooked and unhooked a bra with snap tips, like popping corks. She rented herself out to patriot moms while they were away. And there was a woman with a hairnet named Leona who received "voice mail", meaning calls from loved ones out there, even far out, overseas. A spiritualist thing, Mom said. She had a satellite dish on the roof and talking heads on her TV even when it was off. Other people lit Yankee candles in jars, smoke sticks against bats. They passed biker mags around, a mail-order gun catalogue. Some had army posters, or a border patrol sign: Shadow Wolves. There were sniffy dogs, chicken coops, pumpkin heads. A trailer sold remembrance wreaths. They'd grown heirloom tomatoes in summer, big uglies. The straggly plants still drooped in their cages.

We made it home, back to our clutter. Mom wasn't a housekeper, she just moved things around. Hangers on rails, money she kept in an ottoman, which was a hollow footstool, beauty gizmos rolled around in drawers. We used to have a cat, Beastie, but it got run over. We lost things in the shag rug. Cobwebby hair blew about, secondhand smoke from customers' cigarettes, since we'd moved the swivel chair indoors, pushing stuff out of the way, dollar store wigs hung from clothespins. The damp seeped in, as if the river was coming up under us. And our furniture just sort of piled up. A spongy couch from the Goodwill store, my pullout bed, a cat cushion, thrift shop curtains, an old mantelpiece with a tick-tock clock Mom had picked up at an auction, now collapsing on us, didn't bother us since we were planning to clear out any day now, leaving it all behind. We'd been saving up, in the ottoman and shoe pockets, for our next life, Mom said, on the road, as soon as her songs were ready. Just waiting for that long distance call. Meantime we were in and out. The floor creaked like old bones, the screen door flapped, with a body-shaped dent in the wire mesh from Dad's last visit, when he'd walked into it. We heard sounds in the crawl space underneath, you could almost see through the paper-thin walls, which let in shadows, but we got into a good mood, just the two of us, enjoying some "quality time". Like kids, making faces in the mirror, fitting on wigs, which came naturally to us since we'd been kids together, Mom wasn't much older than me now when she'd had me. Silly girlie things, trying to do an Afro on my woolly hair, always in knots. Flitting along, with a few decorator touches, we hung out a pumpkin lantern, spray-painted a dead bush. Or, feeling homey, Mom baked cupcakes, a big improvement over the diet jello puddings we were on most of the time since she'd been worrying about putting on weight. I almost missed the frozen pizzas we used to buy. Gemma made yogurt ice-cream in a churn. She brought some by and we ate it with soggy cookies, watching a stupid TV show with canned laughs. Blinkety-blink for a while, or we messed around with the electric keyboard, which did beats and could imitate different instruments. We liked the eerie vibraphone best. Then we went and sat out on the porch. Blowing hot and cold, wrapped in a bedspread. At nightfall, with the birds twittering in the trees. Starlings raining down, barn swallows turning into bats, swooped by on silent wings. A moonflower climbed up our wall, just crinkly leaves at this time of the year, but it still seemed to give out a scent, or maybe it was the sickly sweet smell of garbage strewn by coons. Things looming out there, shapes and noises. We heard the water pump going, any time somebody flushed or showered, sloshy river water rising into the tank above the park. The coin wash with its rusty rooftop fan blew hot lint our way. Another time it was the drug bust chopper raising a wind. Hanging over us with its flapping rotors, it shot out a searchlight beam while guys in jumpsuits dropped down a rope ladder. We thought they were the space invaders. There were boomboxes, off and on, in the open and walled in. Hard beats sending shock waves or just a heart throb. The Waikiki ukulele music floated by with a voice singing "Sweet Leilani, heavenly flower". It made Mom's mind wander, way out somewhere. We sat there hanging on. A kind of strangeness came down on us, as if we were already moving on, into our next life. We'd had that feeling ever since I could remember. Mom with her skirt spread out on the steps. Her shoes kicked off because her feet swelled. Half gone, it seemed, but listening to everything, soaking it up, bone deep. We heard a train going by along the track across the river, a clanking beast dragging a long tail. It was a freight train, but we'd heard migrants hopped rides on it. We tried to count the cars by the clicks of the wheels. After about a hundred we gave up, but Mom, who believed in magic numbers, said there were three hundred and sixty five, one for each day of the year. Next we heard a churchbell in town striking time. The gongs bounced around the buildings, bong-along, coming and going.

Once we counted to thirteen, military time, "thirteen hundred hours", you said. Midnight was Zero Hour, a black hole, where only flashes of things reached us, zaps of bug zappers, snapping clotheslines, a spark of lightning on an antenna. It all made a kind of space music, a song that Mom picked up, humming to herself, it went right through her, and up my spine. Easy at first, but then she was breathing hard with her gummy lungs, gasping for air. Smelly dust and smoke blew in from the quarry and the dump. We felt the muddy river weighing on us. A foggy night brew rising, lapping by. I imagined the churning water wheel of the mill upstream. Mom said it was the spin of the world going round and round. A soft breeze that could become a dark wind. She felt her panic attack coming. Shut herself in the house with a bright light on. But she saw spots like dirt in the light. Wheezed and panted and had to use my inhaler. And then she was gone somewhere, out of herself. Like when Dad threatened her and she "wasn't there", floating up above or disappearing into her shadow. She'd learned to do that once when she'd been tied up and gagged. In a previous life just before me. I'd heard her tell Gemma about it. And it was in her hush hush song. That hollowed-out feeling. I'd grab her, but she kept saying: "I'm not in". Sometimes she caught herself in time, sat blowing into her cupped hands, as if to keep a small fire going. But then the phone rang. Dad, she was sure, coming to bash our brains in. She let it ring and ring, or unhooked and hung up again. I listened and didn't hear anything, but we had to get out. With Gemma, who had cabin fever, we drove along the strip, in the middle of the night, to the all-night Giant. We liked it out there, mixing in with the late shoppers, "bag people". Strays like us, of unknown background, bums with foodstamps, little old ladies who lived on hash or pet food, a hooker Gemma knew buying an energy drink, her low-slung guy soft-shoeing after her. Goodies all around. Fighting off cravings, we moved in a sort of white haze, gases from plastic wraps, freezer frost, misty sprays on vegetables, good for breathing. Glass cases lighted up for us, little crispy crackers of sound everywhere, sudden flameouts. Up and down the aisles, homeless and free. Mom drunk on the musak no one else heard, singing along with it. I did a moon walk shuffle with the soft-shoe guy. There was a weightwatchers scale and a post with an armband and a pump where Mom measured her blood pressure, which she was nervous about. Camera eyes spied on us, you saw them blink. Gemma said the rest room had a one-way mirror. We ran into billowy women pushing roller walkers, creeps with peephole eyes, lost in some horny dream, Gemma said, as if they had antlers. I knew lonely souls who bought themselves greeting cards, shoplifters with bulging pockets, the Wonder Bread man in a colored cape like a parasol, a preacher who chanted: "Daylight saving!" Always somebody raving about something. Once I saw two guys necking in a corner. Another slept under a counter. I heard they'd found one stuffed in a trash can. A whale of a man who couldn't hold his own weight rode around on a motorized cart. He wore stretch clothes and an animal house cap. When he came charging up the aisle he reminded me of Dad.

9

I went looking for Dad. Any time I could bike or hitch a ride out. Once I thought I'd heard his voice on the phone: "That you, Buddy?" It sounded like an appeal.

Mom was doing a sleep cure, she forgot about me for days, so I was free to roam, up trails and backwoods, Camp Liberty could be almost anywhere, it was all around us. I'd found different ways in, across the tracks that shunted back and forth behind Stoner's grain elevator in Elton, or following Shit Creek through the hog pens and the chicken farm, or edging past the power relay station with the DANGER. HIGH VOLTAGE sign. Or you could just fall in somewhere, over a ditch or riding an old rail rut, suddenly you'd be up against a gun jammed in your ribs. I watched for signs in unmarked places, like those roadside mailboxes with the flag up but no house in sight, where people came out of nowhere to pick up their mail and vanished again. I'd been out with Keefer the one-armed mailman on his rural delivery route, which he could manage because of the right-hand steering wheel that allowed him to drive along the shoulder and reach through the window, and he said some of the mailboxes were drop-off points. A family called Godlove had an up-and-down cross on the box instead of a flag. Mom's chum, the car rental guy, Mort Damon, took me around sometimes on the taxi runs he did on the side carting "bag ladies" home from the supermarket. I'd heard he also did runs for a lifeline that hid fugitives in churches. And I rode the highway with Jay Bard and Chad, who said they were on a strike force.

Things heated up, as it got colder. We had fog and ice and the first snow days. I knew some Avengers, scouts with dirt bikes, piggybacked on them through the fields, lurching along, with goggles and saddle sores, a bandit scarf tied over my nose. We left muddy tracks and our steamed-up shapes in the air, got bogged and tramped onward in muck boots and puffed-up Michelin jackets and mitts, joined the big guys. There was a surge, they called it. More and more people sneaking in before winter, and more guys signing up to catch them, from around town and the whole county, firemen, road gangs, field hands, even ski bums from Two Top. We followed stalkers, trackers in jeeps and dune buggies. Diggers and other payloaders pitched in, snow plows, steam shovels. Guys grown to twice their size, Mom said, breaking out of their small selves into a bigger life. We'd seen them at worship, stretched sky-high, free spirits singing "Land of the Brave". Others were headhunter types in warpaint, or action heroes spreading "shock and awe", they wore the words in a tattoo. Sniffer dogs pointed the way. Or some twitchy "seer" in a blaze vest, dragging us along. The bucks in camos with their antlers, sounding bullhorns. Some body shop guys in their grease-monkey outfits, like zip-up furs. There were tractors on tank treads, armored with scrap metal from the junkyards. Pirate banners and custom flags flew by. The firefighters with their waterhoses like flamethrowers. We crawled through minefields, under barbed wire, took potshots at the buzzard crows. Snake men helped us, and some friendly survivalists who'd been hoarding weapons with their supplies. Sometimes a duster plane sent a signal, a chopper hovered overhead like a hawk. It could be a medivac or UN parachutists landing on us, or the network news. We shot out flares, tracers, searchlights into the fog. Burst through thickets, jumped ditches. There was a command and control center somewhere, we saw transmission towers cutting a swath through the trees. Ghost lights, which meant wisps of swamp gas burning off, though that was supposed to happen only in summer, so maybe it was rotten bodies or a blowout, there were different theories. We sighted a blimp or a weather balloon over a meadow, maybe an air drop. We heard echoing shots from a rifle range at the foot of the ski slope, where guys wearing earmuffs did target practice with human cutouts. The duster planes, which normally wouldn't be working until spring, sprayed bug spray, "pest control". A freezing cold sun became a blinding snowstorm. We fell into mudholes and snowdrifts. Dropped out, with chills and sweats, but came back. Our hunters' sixth sense led us on, like the sky compass of migrating birds Dad had once told me about, which was stronger than even the global positioning system. We followed the traces of things left behind, plastic bottles, bits of discarded clothing, a whiff of campfire ashes: "They can't be far!" At times we caught glimpses of them: "flashers" running through a field, ducking into a drift. We plunged in after them, set raging dogs on them, pit bulls or any old mutt with a growl. At one point, in a jeep, we picked up a guy, tied him in his sleeves, took him along to show us the way to a hideout, then dumped him in a ditch. Other guys burrowed like sewer rats. In the dark we ran over somebody, we felt the bump. On and on, wearing them down. Those already caught we left in bundles, bound hands and feet, thrashing around, out on the edge of the road, to be hauled off by dump trucks and stored in the Gift storage units behind the railyard until they could be disposed of. Some broke loose and ran blinded into headlights, crossing a highway, jumped into a stream, had to be fished out. I saw them carrying children and old people on their backs, dropping and dragging them, the kids leaving snow angels.

One campsite was in a sort of crater, likely one of those holes made by space invaders when they landed. They'd barricaded themselves behind an outcropping, clawing over mounds of rubble. We beamed lights and loud music at them, threw smoke bombs, a flash bang grenade. A chopper made its whirl above, like a huge ceiling fan. I heard bulldozers working, Deeres and Caterpillars hulking in the dark. It got late and wet. There'd been a thaw, there was a stormy moon. We began to see those swamp lights around us. Another time a Hollerer patriot saw a flaming bush, heard a voice from Bald Mountain. Some prayer warriors sang "Hope and Glory", where it said we were God's country. I was with the Avengers, now a mobile field force, revving up, and we went backfiring into the dark, chased figures that slipped away, and got lost and ended up with some survivalists, who let us in an electric fence and across a moat into their reinforced concrete bunker, where they said they were holding out against the Feds.

10

Things got worse. It was all-out war, all winter, with no let-up. A windy, cold winter, with slick roads, blizzards that brought down power lines, whiteouts. Guys jerked out of body shops, bars, the Game Stop at the mall, where they fought battles on screens, Wally's Exxon, which went self-serve. Cops signed up, mailmen, a hairdresser we knew at the spa on the strip, scumbags from the Lion's Den, truckers at the Big Rig truck stop. Flophouse bums, off the street, joined the home guard. All throwing their weight around. Man tan wrestlers and body beautiful builders. The safety patrol tore up and down the roads, causing blackouts when they skidded into a utility pole. Girls rode "bareback" along with bronco buster bikers. In school there were kids without dads or moms or both, gone on endless tours of duty. They played war games, picking on the camper kids, kneed them and tripped them up in the hallways. Fast-draw guys called Trig, Ammo, or Bible names like Levi, which was also a show-off label, like their Barbie girls, blonde bombshells and beauty queens, who listened to death rap, which was horror movie music, all about murder and rape.

I drove around with Jay Bard and Chad or sat up at night with Mom. In a while the ground shook, fire trucks rushed by to put out a blaze somewhere. We tailed them with Gemma in her Camaro. Pounding bells on the highway, a burning farmhouse. Once a silo had blown up. At first we thought the explosion was a crew blasting rock in the quarry. And they caught people climbing out of a culvert, maybe terrorists tunneling in like moles. And so on, night and day. Sightings, raids, firefights. Then the guys coming back all beat-up, staggering around, an arm or a leg gone. Many of them shutmouthed, wouldn't talk about it. Still out there in their heads, gone missing even when they were home. Kicking around the house, brooding. You could hear them ticking like time bombs. And suddenly they lost it, broke out of a nightmare howling, hit a wall, then sank back in a cold sweat. They had rallies, a torch-lit march for fallen heroes. Swearings and invocations at the animal houses, with their songs and cheers. The Hollerers babbling, some gifted kid chanting. Moments of silence, inspirational music. They wore empty holsters. Just exercising their right to bear arms. Some old guy out of a nursing home wheezed words of wisdom. We had our spies, Becky and Lori Lipp who'd been a harelip, the gash still showed, and spoke through her nose, but that didn't stop her, and Kenya, a little black Barbie, dressed out of a kit, all "anatomically correct", and pretty as a picture, in cornrows with twisties, who talked blank talk. At one of the "houses" there was a weekly family night. Supposedly a fun time, but it was more like a wake. All single moms, or dads, when the mom was the warrior. A preacher carried on about the dearly departed. He said there were a lot more of them than us. He meant all the dead through the ages keeping us company, Becky figured it out. And at Temple Lodge there was a wedding with a "white widow": a war bride in a mourning veil. They stood the groom up in a casket and she put a wreath on him. He wore a waxy funeral home mask of his own face and shiny curls, lacquered. Joe Marvel's airport limo waited outside, and a row of cars with burglar alarms, they honked every time somebody got in or out.

At Rosie's with Mom we heard stories. Truckers told of things they'd seen on the road, UFOs that raised gale force winds, a flash flood, on one of the crazy-weather warm days we had between freezes, hail storms and low pressures that shattered windshields, an airhole that sent a plane into a tailspin. Fighters, working on their plate-size steaks and crab legs still crawling and clawing at them, brought tales of rivers of fire, guys who threw themselves on exploding shells to save their buddies. Making up for lost time with the girls, they dropped dumb jokes like lead balloons. On karaoke nights they had singalongs. The Cowboy Saloon had changed its name. Now it was the Canteen, with a Welcome banner across the front for the citizen army. There was a bikers' dive nextdoor, and the Silk Screen, a noodle house where overseas veterans with "take-home" girls hung out. Mom and

Gemma sang with whatever back-up they could get, twanging guitars, a juke with a beat. They'd ask for a track and do the vocals. Once they billed themselves as the Merry Maids, in skimpy aprons. Gemma had a peekaboo number where she popped her butt out to show she was wearing a thong. Mom tried some down home stuff. The guys blown away, shouting and hooting in their beery haze. Then she went into her singsong, as Gemma called it. A kind of lullaby with dark undertones. Some guys recovering from bad wounds stared wide-eyed but in a dream, you could tell by the way their eyes moved, Mom said. Focused on something out there, or nowhere. Others just looked stoned or spaced out.

11

Dad was back, several times. Banging on the door or slipping in. I'd find him there or have the feeling he was around. Parked somewhere nearby, honking for her. He had a "musical" horn you couldn't miss. Mom's eyes went blank when I asked, but I knew she'd been seeing him on the sly all along. Now snowstorms were interrupting operations. Guys straggled home, and he landed on us. He sprawled on the couch and splashed in the shower. Just for a few days, until there was a break in the weather: "That okay with you, Buddy?" Jittery as usual, watching his tail, he ran to hide back out in the weeds when somebody called that he didn't know, like a meter man, who could be a government agent. He dozed fitfully, afraid of falling asleep and having something creep up on him or worse, he told me, of what he might do in his sleep, without being able to stop himself, tear up the house or rush out and kill somebody. Like the other big guys, aching to get back to war. Dreaming of it and cracking up, Gemma said. Waking in a sweat that felt like a bloodbath. And it might come on him at any time, even wide awake. Heaving and pitching all day, jumping out of his skin. He sat in the rocker, waving things away. Or sunk into himself, brooding mightily. He hit the deck when he heard tires on the gravel, or just the Hawaiian coming by to collect the rent. He thought thunder was machine gun fire. Listened for calls, steps, rustling branches, anything that stirred, his own clothes or parts of his body that moved as if they didn't belong to him. Pings in the walls. He said the house was bugged. It was some kind of mind control. On the porch swing, lovey-dovey with Mom one minute, on one of those days of balmy weather, suddenly he'd start hyperventilating, like Gemma said, and work himself up into a fit again. He went wild when a camper van with dark windows drove past on the road. Leaped up slamming his fist into the air, yelling, choking on his spit. Once he punched a hole through the wall. He pissed off the edge of the porch, went off to eat in the truck. Mom was so scared of him that she "wasn't there", just floated away somewhere, out of reach. Days before, she felt him coming. Even if he didn't turn up, there'd be "voice mail" from him, we'd find his stuff lying around. Mom said he left his hair everywhere, like a cat or a bear. He called from a disposable cell phone that ran on a card or a chip or something that faded out before he got through, bawling in the distance. Sometimes he'd be in a party mood, he went out to raise hell with the guys, at Rosie's or the Barn, if it was a V-Day, singing "Country First". Other times he was the backslapper, joking with the neighbors, shooting hoops with the kids, whistling for pets. At a baby baptism he sprinkled everyone with a trick flower in his buttonhole, squeezing a rubber bulb in his pocket. He was great at greeting customers: "Have a seat, lovely lady!", made motions to help Mom with her chores, instead of lazying around. A big build-up of good will, boiling over with it. He took me fishing through a hole in the ice. A spot where the river was still frozen, in spite of the spring thaw, a week earlier I'd been footskating on it. We caught a toothy fish we called Jaws. He said in summer he'd hooked a jellyfish but couldn't show me because it had melted away. He brought me war trophies, a spent bullet or a lucky bone. The little keepsakes he bribed me with. Once he dropped some bobs. I thought they were eyeballs. On a windy day we went kite-flying in a pasture with half buried headstones, an old battlefield cemetery. He'd made the kite himself, out of plywood and silk paper, a miracle glue miracle, light as a butterfly, snapping up in the sky as it caught the wind and took off, with a comet tail and a tug that almost tore us off our feet, like souls soaring. On our way back we stopped at an ostrich farm where they also kept a llama, which was like a small woolly camel and spat at us.

Then with Mom we had a "night on the town". A big spending spree he took us on, at a Spirits and Fine Dining restaurant in a business park, a classy place, cocktails in a lounge, low lights and soft music and steak and seafood, the works. We went in style, in a borrowed Grand Prix. He wore a pink striped jacket and a flashy tie and Mom an uppity bra that

showed through her lacy dress. We stopped on our
way to have our picture taken at Photo Gem, he'd
won a coupon for a free family portrait in a raffle.
I had to wear a sissy dress with titty puckers. They
looked like they were in a wedding picture. I was
Little Miss Sweetheart. All I needed was a pouty
lollipop. Another time he took us on a joyride in the
dump truck, out toward Two Top. He knew a shortcut
through town, riding a train track for a block, then
wham-bang across some car lots, and we were
off. A furry paw hung over the dash with a picture
postcard of Bigfoot the Snowman. We sailed out into
the wind, past a development with ranch houses he
wanted to show us, where he was going to buy us
a dream home. He waved his arms, while the truck
steered itself. Then he let me steer, seated on his lap. I
blew the horn, which played "Woody Woodpecker".
On a high, both of us. Through a thunderstorm that
turned into hail the size of mothballs and cleared,
like his moods. The deep-set hills out ahead in lights
and shadows, others misty behind them. Mom going
along, to humor us, she let on, but she began to enjoy
herself, laughed and sang with the radio. We made it
all the way to Overlook, headed for the lake resort,
where you could rent an outboard, but suddenly he
went into one of his rages over nothing: "I'm outta
here!" and dumped us on the road, ten, twelve miles
from home, soaking in the rain, which had started
again, our smart dresses a mishmash, good thing we
were going downhill, and a rig picked us up when
we'd walked halfway home.

12

He disappeared again. Great news and to hell with him, Mom said, she'd got a court order against him. Gemma drove her to the hearing. They said he'd be notified. Still in dread of him certain days, locked in behind our shutters and mothy curtains, we hid from the streaks of light, as if they were his eyes watching us though the thin walls. We spent whole days that way. Rain and fog all around when we stuck our noses out. The sun as pale as the moon. Mom in a panic, gasping for breath. She had to use my asthma spray. We both lay there wheezing. Hard beats pounding outside. The world turning on a noisy hinge. I'd leave her in the dark when I went to school. I got back in fading daylight. She'd been shivering, the heat going like a blast furnace, having locked up after just a couple of overheated customers all day.

But then it was really spring. Even with sprinkles of blossoms in the dead grass. We dug ourselves out.

Mom doing her breathing exercises, when the fertilizer pipes on bird legs weren't spreading their shit in the fields. She walked around the house naked, admired herself in the mirror, as her reflection floated up as if from underwater. Mine, too, growing a body. She said I was budding. The ladies came in for their hair jobs. Foamy shampoos, puffy waves, layered cuts and fantasies. Even men, for pomps or blow-drys. They loved her styles, which she'd learned in a five-week correspondence course from an institute, though basically she made them up herself, copied from charm and beauty mags. She said heads needed airing, like houses. And, when you looked around, everyone was opening wide, beating mattresses, running washers and sweepers. Scarred and battered but fixing up. There was sunny weather. Only a few gusts of wind blew up "tornado alley", where a twister had once cut straight across the park. The flapping awnings, flags, buzzing wires made their song. We got in the mood and walked around, enjoying the sights. The world laid out, trailers all shapes and sizes, on big and small plots, shiny "diners", two-bit shacks, mobiles still on wheels, singles and doubles, a half double in one place, sealed off with tarpaper, breadloaves and boaters, ranchers, rundown luxury motor homes, Airstreams, a Trailblazer, a Riviera on stilts. Mostly tin siding and crabgrass yards, but also cutie underskirts, maybe a corkscrew-shaped bush out front or a patch of phlox or a birdhouse. Thorny berry bushes out our way. But we had a hanging basket on the porch and were planning a vegetable garden, if Dad ever got around to bringing us a load of soil in the dump truck. Some lanes had names, like Maiden Lane. In a Melody lane they sold used records, then they changed to Memory Lane and sold Jack Bargain type junk they called antiques. One path ended in a grape arbor with shady vines. In summer the purple grapes boiled and in autumn they dripped drops of wine or dried out into sugary raisins. Along Sky-Lane there was a wide-bodied home with a deck for cookouts and a view of the town below and the valley, which had a hokey name, La Vale.

We visited or sat out at night. On moonlit nights there were fireflies, chirping crickets, Mom said they had spring fever. You felt a trill in the air. Walked into spiderwebs with dewdrops. Millions of bogey bugs and creatures in each drop, I'd seen them under the microscope in school. She did herself up in a new dress, a Dora Belle. That was the lady who made woman-size dresses, she had her own label. We got around, just picking up vibes. Feeling safe for awhile, even if Dad was stalking us. There was a neighborhood watch, we knew them and roamed with them. Gemma came along, doing her rounds. Door and window stops, hitting on some guy she'd met at the 24-7 convenience store. We'd follow a tracker with a jerky walk, plugged-in guys--"walkmen"-- others carrying "rabbit ears", in touch with out-of-the-way places, a factory nightwatchman on his night off. They could stay up forever, twelve-hour shifts like nothing, just staring out into the dark. There was a guy who sleepwalked in jammies, you couldn't wake him or he'd crash. Plodding down into the ground, deep in a rut, it seemed, he'd walk into a wall, back up and turn and go on until it happened again. Another guy limped on a stump, he said he had a phantom leg. Everyone armed against prowlers, and ready for the Feds if they tried to take our weapons away because of some new gun law. The Hawaiian went around keeping track. The loudspeaker at the office blaring "Sweet Leilani", his siren song to attract customers, Mom said. He called himself Earl, ambled up in lordly fashion, swinging his arms wide. The office signboard flashed neon. Gassy letters blinked on and off. The flag on a pole blew like a windsock. It was always Flag Day or Loyalty Day or whatever. A gaudy sign in the window said ESTATE SALES. INVESTMENT PROPERTIES. Mom used to go there to use the pay phone. I went for the coin machine, and to wipe my shoes on the plush Welcome mat. It was cozy inside, paneling and upholstery. A fireplace glowed with a fake "Yule log". The flames were streams of lights. There was a screen where they monitored movements in the park, it was all mapped out in images. Wide angle mirrors in some alleys saw around corners. Earl sat there, leaning back on springs, hands clasped behind his head, with his strongarm guys, making deals. The music going, ululating, as Mom said. The barrelchested bouncer, Lamar, with a screwed-up pug nose, was the enforcer. A runty guy, known as the broker, was a payday lender, he cashed checks for a fee. Chewing on a stub of a cigar, he granted audiences, propped on a fat cushion like a throne. We'd asked for a loan once. It was like being received at the Keystone Bank. He gave us a clammy hand, pinpoints of shifty eyes watching us, laid out "terms and conditions", took half of it back on the spot as down payment. Another time he wolf-whistled me. I was going by barefoot. Gemma said it made you sexy, unless you had flat feet. Then there was Dag Super, the maintenance man. He ran the water pump, cut it off when we used too much for washing or watering. We also had blackouts to save on power. Brownouts when we wandered in a sort of bug repellent light. I sometimes ran errands for them. Out to the store to buy cigarettes. A gun for hire with the Bosses. They let me keep the change. It was pocket money. Meantime, Mom sang at send-off parties, going-away songs she knew, take-me-with-you songs, don't-be-long songs, she was becoming famous for them, and at birthdays and funerals, hellos and goodbyes, whatever came up, they'd started asking for her. The Hollerers wanted her, too. In the Ark, where they played hymns on a keyboard with amplifiers, she sang solos, with the Angel Choir behind her, and also without back-up, they said she had an aura, which was a light around her, especially when she slipped into her eerie singsong. Gemma thought they were recording her and she ought to charge them for it, a preacher with a pomp called Doctor Holiday even wanted to marry her.

In beween we went to the town fair. Out in the community park. It was a month full of V-Days: Loyalty Day, VE-Day, Armed Forces Day and so on, marching bands, and fun at the fair, games, eats and a carnival, rides, wheels, exhibits. Sponsored by the animal houses. Sheds with picnic tables, a bingo board, music in a band shell. We bought bonus tickets with free rides, good for three days, mixed in with the townies. Mom hoping to meet someone different, maybe pick up new customers, inspired by the success of Dora Belle, who was getting to be known in town for her big lady styles, she wore a beauty hair-do with a glaze I'd helped her put on. Gemma wore a sleazy T-shirt that said: "The secret is out". We threw rings, horseshoes, shot at bottles and dummies, rode the spinning star, a lit mushroom, the music express and a carousel with circus horses and barberpoles to hold on to. Whirled with the world, flew off in every direction. Pigged out on slushies, hot dogs, candied apples, funnel cake and cotton snow. Bounced around on bumper cars, ran through a house of horrors with distorting mirrors, did a taffy pull. We pinned on flag pins and party buttons, because an election was coming up. A clown called Smiley danced off his feet into the air hanging from gas balloons. Gemma won a goldfish in a contest. A guy snatched it from her and swallowed it. A plane did loop-the-loops overhead. Streamers announced a strawberry festival. The Hollerers were there baptizing, not just down in the river anymore. Dunking people in a tub, in the Faith Van, a sign said: "Go whole hog!" And at a first-aid stand they practiced the "kiss of life" on a dummy with a mouthpiece, sort of like Ricky the show-and-tell skeleton in school but made of imitation body parts instead of just bones. Huge noisy machinery everywhere made it all work and go round, big-bird cranes, bone-grinding wheels, generator trucks the size of moving vans. There was an oldtime barker in a side show with zoo animals, a bear in an animal-crackers cage, a freaky giraffe, which was like a tame dinosaur, sticking its neck out to eat leaves off a tree. Mom, who'd been hearing things, said it sang to itself all the time, which

Gemma said was impossible, because giraffes had no voices, she'd read that somewhere. In a Native American exhibit they showed a death head on a pole called Man of God. Some bearded Brethren had a stand where they sold muddy fudge. They were against government. They didn't vote in elections or pay taxes. A mobile kitchen sold "chiliburgers", in a big smoke. I'd never noticed it before. Two laughing lady cooks inside. And at the window a pretty boy my age with thick knit brows, as if deep in thought, gazing at me, till I flipped a bird at him. At night the crowd went shadowy. Leaflets blew in the breeze. People like neon-lit specters, fading and lighting up again, electric ghosts. A rock band in the band shell under a rainbow arch sang: "Born to be free, be all you can be".

13

In those days Dad called, left his sound on the answering machine. I got to it before Mom wiped it off. I'd seen him a couple of times, hanging around. He wanted to make up with Mom, take us to live in Sunnyside. "You tell her, Buddy". Now he'd left just a word: "Trayer's". That meant down by the river, the old pier where we used to meet, below the abandoned apple orchard. So I went and sat awhile over the rotten piles, watching things go by in the slow current, trash snagged on dead branches, sinking logs. A shadow under the surface might be a swimmer making his way along the bottom. Some decoy-like ducks drifted by. There were bathers, baptists wading in, a bum taking a crap in the bushes, but no Dad. Mom said he was on the run again.

Then he wanted us to meet along the road to Cove Gap, didn't say exactly where, he'd look out for me, signal me somehow. Tiny Tina took me out in the

special-ed school minibus with Becky and the other
gifted kids, Lori Lipp and Mae Sung, a "take-home"
kid with a genius IQ, and a baldy with a veiny skull,
like a jailbird, and a camper kid who heard voices
on his Walkman and threw his arms around going
"Bang! Bang!" Tiny Tina was the special-ed school
bus driver, so-called because she could barely get
her nose over the dash, even with the driver's seat
jacked up as high as she could raise it and still reach
the pedals, from the outside it looked like the bus
was driving itself with its flashers, STOP sign and
folding door. I used to ride the bus, because of my
asthma, back in the days when the attacks were
so bad that they thought I had some kind of brain
disease. We went out to houses and farms, making
stops and starts, keeping watch. Becky sat next to
me. We linked pinkies. She'd been teaching me finger
counting. She was chewing on a pacifier, as she did
when she was nervous. Otherwise she might bite her
tongue or tear out her hair in clumps. She told me
she'd dreamed of a whale. It kept singing her name,
which was Abigail, through its blowhole. Dad could
be anywhere, they said he had another family--and
another me?-- which I was curious about. Miles out,
where moms waited at lone mailboxes so their kids
wouldn't be kidnaped by some maniac or run over.
There were crosses along the edge of the road where
there'd been accidents, some with names on them
and a posy or a wreath. One was a fence post that
had branched out and flowered, over a little chapel
with a glittery saint inside. Bang Bang the camper
kid got off there. In some places it was just a sign that
said "Come back". Celebration signs, Tiny Tina said,

for Pentecost. She tuned in on her stereo. A revival station played comeback music. It broadcast from a barn with a New Life hex on the loft.

I stayed on all the way, till we reached the county line, where we turned around, backing into a drive, and still no Dad. "Missing in action", like Mom said men usually were. Yet we felt his hairy presence in the house, when she started panting and had to get into her breathing aid, a sort of bellows she strapped on like a life jacket. Gemma working on her, and my asthma making me hyperventilate, which could also be an out-of-body experience, when I thought of him. Though I suspected Mom was still seeing him in secret. I'd get home and find boot treads on the carpet, a caved-in spring in the couch. But maybe it was some guy who'd come in for a hairpiece. An iron-pumping muscleman, pecs big as tits, but beginning to sag, going flabby with grief, I'd seen a few of those, falling all over her. She met them at Rosie's or some "coffee for gossip" diner. Swinging on a stool, sharing a joint with Gemma, who treated them rough. But Mom listened to them, sang them to sleep, or just held and rocked them, in a sweet smoke, while they spilled out some sob story, and chances were one of them would end up parked outside our trailer at night, gunning the motor. One guy went around metering radon. That was a kind of underground radiation. Glinty-eyed and with a flaring beard, like some wizard or mastermind, Mom fell for that. She said he had uncanny vision. They talked about other worlds. He'd visited one, Dulcimer, in a space ship like a spinning top. You went through a sort of donut hole to get there. He said there was the energy of divinity in each of us, it made his meter tick. He was a skydiver, had Mom half convinced for awhile, but she discovered he smelled of burned flesh, as if he'd been hit by lightning, and he showed us one day, baring his back, crusts of charred skin all over, with red hot sores.

Lots of guys like that, coming back all broken. Goners, Gemma called them. Roaming wild-eyed, throwing a long shadow. Burned, crippled, limbs and faces blown off, cracked heads. Leaning on each other or on crutches, wheeled along on wheelchairs. Any one of them could be Dad, in a sweaty fury, as the weather got steamy, barging through doors, like stags or bears driven out of the woods by a drought or fire. Barely surviving on odd jobs or disability. Useless bags of bones, some of them, or strangers, they'd been away for so long, years sometimes, that no one recognized them, they didn't know themselves who they were, stumbled into the wrong trailer, wearing somebody else's face or clothes, maybe looking for a family that had moved out or reorganized without him. "Went by, weren't no one there". Lost as if they were still gone, prowling in the woods, disguised as crawling bushes or antler heads, listening for hoots and cries. Top-heavy bodies in faded combat fatigues, their wounds another camouflage. A war stress sickness was going around. Guys with their minds shot, you saw them stalking their own shadows or balled up in a corner, sweating bullets. Hiding out, many of them, like Dad, from the Feds or the Blue Helmets. They had nightmares, reliving their bad memories, flashbacks, Gemma said, woke up startled and fired out the window. Gemma was working on phantom limbs, which were missing arms or legs that ached or cramped as if they were still there, tore you apart, she used a "mirror therapy" where she made a guy flex his one leg in the mirror, pretending it was the other one. She had guys on stumps, and there was the sleepwalker you couldn't wake. Seeing-eye guys chasing their visions, mummies trailing bandages as if their skin was peeling off. Fighter girls, too, I saw one squatting in a pool of blood, in a shed, having a baby. Pigeons were making a feathery mess around her. And she came out cooing but cradling just her own arms, wrapped in rags. A guy all scarred and sewed up joked about being bionic, he had so many replacement parts, joints, kneecaps, a piece of skull, he couldn't be sure he was still the same person, moved about clicking like a robot, lucky he worked at the army depot, where they kept spares. Others "followed the music", like Mom said, meaning the sound of Welcome Home parties with banners stretched across alleys, garlands of hearts and messages, even in empty houses, like one I knew on a ledge, where they'd left all the lights on until they burned out and the house went dark, but a strand of winged letters like notes in a loony tune cartoon still said: "Love you wherever you are".

14

I rode out with Chad and Jay Bard. In their bucking bronco pick-up with a hood scoop like flared nostrils. Shotgun, over the power train, or was it the crank shaft, which was which? Chad at the wheel, doing his jerks and starts, he'd once shot a deer and jumped on and rode it till it died. We tore up trails through parched fields. They looked weathered, great strong sun-baked guys with the scars of outdoor life, maybe battle wounds, like the scab Jay had up one arm where he'd been stitched after an accident with a chain saw at the sawmill, and Chad had been running laps in a sprint car on the speedway. Not smelling of sod and dung like they used to but some smooth aftershave that drove girls crazy, grown-up, and me too, in a tank top they appreciated.

We rode around on recon checking out all the places we knew, runs, hollows, woods, the crumbling quarry with the swimming hole where we'd once gone skinny-dipping in the moonlight, now dried out, the pimply frogs and even the lizards in the rocks dead as dinosaurs. It was a blazing hot fall, everything laid waste, patches of crops ripped out, creeks gone off in vapors, barns catching fire, silos blowing up, because of global warming, which everyone talked about, a complete meltdown, scrapped equipment all over the place, pieces of tractors, guns, muscle cars, even a tank, whole tracts of land like junkyards. We saw a cannon stuck in a rut, like a rocket landed on its nose. Salvagers in dump trucks scavenged parts, batteries, mufflers, leaky radiators, for a chop shop. Bumper stickers said: "Hell and back". A busted world down to bare bones. We saw it smoking from the outlook at Indian Head. The sky faded in the blinding light, the trees cracking, split down the middle, with raw cables running through them. We headed out toward Bald Mountain, Bigfoot stomping ground. Huge tracks led into Land's End, an old strip mine, where the earth glowed like embers. A wind blew tinny dust with sparks, probably the radioactive fallout we'd been warned about. Once we spotted some wildflowers in the scrub, we couldn't believe it, Jay Bard said: "Must be somebody buried underneath". And there were swamp lights around the reservoir, those gases from rotting bodies. Fishy smells from a fish farm. Patrols still roved, making death-metal noise, loose groups mopping up. Some were still burning scarecrow crosses, straw men like souls going up in flames. They torched hideouts and bulldozed abandoned campsites. We found the scorched remains of a charter bus that had once been inhabited, with burned tires piled high over it. A sooty rain fell on us. Earthmovers were plowing up farmland for developments, turning drainage pipes into sewers. The buzzard crows winged overhead. Skyhawks, Jay Bard said, copters in the distance. Screeching gulls with singed wings hung over dumps and landfills. A lone jack pumped in an empty oilfield, like some long-neck monster. Only the survivalists were left, holding out in their bunker, which used to be a missile silo, surrounded by razor wire and a moat, where you saw them on manure spreaders, with secret tunnels to move goods through, hoarding arms and provisions that could last them years, others up on a watchtower, shooting at trespassers and ready to take on the Feds if they tried to smoke them out.

It was noisy downtown. Tailgate parties in parking lots, gang bashes, pickets. There were miners on a strike, blackface guys with lamps on their foreheads, up from an underground flood or explosion. War protesters had a march. Then laid-off workers from a "smokestack" factory. Churches ran disaster relief. Godly forces calling themselves Saints, Friends, Brothers. The patriots held a rally, with bullhorn speeches from a bucket on a boom lift. It was another V-Day. Mom didn't want to miss out. We rode the new county bus into town. Full of "bag ladies" but light as air, it ran on batteries. Another time we nosed down the slope in one of Mort Damon's rental cars, he'd started a regular taxi service. All headed in the same direction, bikers on their crotch rockets, schoolbuses. Butting into each other in the streets, as if locking horns. It went on for days, in a dirty sun, grimy nights. Mom kept me awake. She dragged me through the bars, wouldn't let go. She said she felt a huge heart beating, running on. There was music everywhere, sirens, church bells, honking cars, all mixed up. Flower girls on a float one day, petals flying like feathers out of burst pillows. It was a homecoming parade with school bands. All the animal houses took part, the Elks, Moose, Lions, the Bears, the Kiwanis, which sounded like a Hawaiian animal. Fraternal orders, firemen, mounted police, whatever, the home guard, Native American hawks and eagles in warbonnets, the Mountain Men militia, rolling thunder bikers, Angels and Predators, veterans in wheelchairs, hunters wearing racks, bums from the Sigmar Hotel, oldies from Elder Care. There were fireworks that sounded like shootouts. The tower clock struck its military gong. "Historic monument" buildings lit up. The bands played Superbowl music. A Bloodmobile or Vampire Van went around. Rams dangling balls from their tow hitches. I cruised with Jay Bard and Chad. Squeezed in between them, "cheek to cheek", calling out bumper stickers and license plates: "Freedom Fighter", "Desert Storm". There was a reenactment of a battle scene, a great photo-op. Paratroopers landed on the square like bungee jumpers, from a rooftop construction crane. Masters of the Universe! They beat down an enemy position and posed with the wreck. The fountain spread rainbow colors. A preacher stood in it, baptizing. Billboard trucks blared, pole vaulters did backflips. In a minute of silence for a Salute a cannon boomed. It was a fighter jet up above going "sonic", part of an air show with two more jets that did nose dives and left spirals of steam. The Hollerers pitched their Old Glory tent on the fairgrounds. Ran it up wires, billowing out in the breeze. They called it the Big

Top. They sang All-Souls and Saints-Marching-In hymns. Smiley the clown, in a Batman cloak, played the Devil. Mummers danced across a bridge: a faceless group, "We the People". Kids wearing pumpkin heads. Another time, they carried a witch on a broomstick and a rattling skeleton. There was a zombi, which was a black ghost. That would be Frisbee, the shadow boy, lord of the underworld. We did a hoodoo-voodoo stomp. I was a ghoul from Hell, with Dracula teeth and bat wings.

Mom was wound up, out of herself. Seeing and hearing things, voices, thoughts that became songs, I heard them in my mind. A wind started up, caught us in its whiplash. I walked her around with Gemma. We had to hold her up between us so she wouldn't fold. Back in Waikiki Heights a dust devil spun leaves up our alley. Blowing and howling, as if the slow coal train on the tracks below had somehow picked up speed and was rolling over us. We slogged through a mess of flying garbage and rotted pawpaws fallen from a ragged tree. Waves seemed to burst around us: the river washing up gurgling drains. We tried to sleep it off at home, but woke before dawn. Mom felt a pull, she drew me along with her, in whirls of dead leaves, up to our knees. We followed a home brewery smell, in the bug-repellent light. A Dreamboat had overturned, spilling out over an edge where there was a drop down to the embankment. A family and neighbors were climbing all over it, lit by headlights, in a kind of mad glee, some hanging backward, holding it with ropes, a cable from a winch in a tow truck, and a boozy guy who'd been flapping his arms, beating his sides, jumped off the roof as if he could fly, down a zip line.

15

We'd seen a turkey strut by with its tail feathers fanned out. A guy bred them for Thanksgiving. Fat toms and hens, twenty-pounders. Raised "free range", they came gobbling at you, stretching out their wrinkly necks as if talking in tongues. Mom said they had the gift of gab. At one of the animal houses they made a great to-do about granting a Tom Turkey a pardon and getting the picture in the paper. A talk show had one on the show, "Talking Turkey", and a special forces guy we knew who owned carrier pigeons wanted to train turkeys as messenger birds.

Some kids held a Turkey Day celebration at the campground. They'd bagged a wild bird. Undercover because the season had closed. A breasty drummer with a fancy beard. Obviously thought a lot of himself. They addressed him as Your Holiness. His plucked wings and wattle flared up when they roasted him on a spit. They'd left his head on so he could call out. They sat around the fire and smoked a peace pipe. I went with Frisbee, who could make us invisible. We'd got hold of some applejack. Gemma made it in her freezer. It sent you straight into the spirit world. There were patriot kids and others, all sorts, some from the mountains or dirt farms, you never saw them the rest of the year. Hollerer kids who'd been barnstorming. Hunter kids wearing their racks. And fighters bragging of their war deeds. You wouldn't believe it, but one had caught a spy in a cage trap, another had laid mines, a whiz kid had invented some weapon of mass destruction. A kid who'd had surgery said he was an organ donor. And show-off girls writhed. Some with cramps, having their curse, others the big bang, moaning and faking it. It was like a fire dance. We chanted Indian chants. Becky sang an "almighty". She was there, too. And Butterball, who broke out and sang a hero tale. Heads bobbing with him, not like in school, where he was a punching bag. The Hollerer kids witnessing and prophesying. Pilgrim kids and "Indians" with feather headdresses, all under the spell. Even a few gypsy camper kids. Huddled nearby, hanging on to each other, wearing hoodies, staying out of sight. Some kids called the cannibals, celebrating a feast of theirs that happened to coincide with Thanksgiving, gave out bead necklaces. The beads were eyes and teeth. And I wore my dust mask. Dead leaves blew about. They rattled like bird scarers. The Waste Management truck went by on the road, which was strange on a holiday, it smelled of jet fuel. I imagined moonies jumping off, in capes like dark wings. Some kids who'd been shying around, shivering in the cold, moved in with us. Runaways, out of the tarps where they hid out. They wore head socks, but I recognized them, from the times when I'd had to run from home. Loners, most of the time, but they gathered regularly because of a kid buried there, under the trees. They'd found him in a spring thaw and dug his grave. Only they knew about him. Then the special kids came on. Dummies but who transmitted things. A girl did a honeybee dance, over and over, like a wind-up toy, and there was a kid born without arms, because of chemical contamination, but who got his message across with his flippers, and the runaways knew turkey cries, which they used for signals among themselves, kee-kee calls, yelps and clucks, and Becky gave her "godbless", spinning like a windmill.

Mom was in bed when I got home, she'd slept all day, and made me climb in next to her. But then she woke me in the dark, assing me out over the edge because she thought Dad was in there with us.

16

I was learning to drive. Whizzing along in the Four By Four with the JB Landscaping boys. They'd hand me the wheel on side roads: "Floor it, Angie!" and I took off. They had power drive, which made it easy, I just had to hang on and steer. Before I knew it I was doing 80, yippee-ki-yay! Honking and tailgaiting: "Out of my way!" Slamming on the power brakes at stops. Around hairpin curves, hayloads on wheels, roadside bombs, traffic cones, or "riding herd" crosscountry, flushing out wildlife, there was nothing I couldn't do.

Then one day, when I wasn't even thinking about him, I saw Dad's truck ditched by the highway, just outside our speed bump. Slumped there, lopsided but undamaged, no flats or signs of a smash-up. The furry paw still hanging over the dash, the key in the ignition. Mom had been saying he'd skipped town. A fast getaway, not one you'd use a truck for. And she didn't drive, since she couldn't stand the glare on the windshield, because of laser surgery she'd had done on one eye at the mall, so he must have left it for me. Without a note or anything, I looked everywhere. But I found my picture in the glove compartment. An old dog-eared photo, I didn't even recognize myself. A little naked girlie with a big belly button, in a splash of water, drinking from a hose. Still tubby, not gawky, the way I was now, but it said "Buddy" in back. I could hear him calling. I climbed in, let out the brake, got the engine going, managed the shift and the clutch, which I'd practiced when I used to ride on his lap, stepping on his feet, turned out on the road, which was clear at the moment, and rolled downhill, with almost no gas, just enough to gear down and hold, bucking and blowing music on the horn, all the way into town, with some noisy kids who'd jumped on behind bugging me, banging on the roof. Around a last bend, I went through a stoplight and wound up between two trees, a wheel on the sidewalk and another jammed against the curb. There was a cop cruiser across the street, but in traffic and headed the other way. I got off and walked. The kids behind me, a townie gang, acquaintances. Slick chicks and hotshots shoving up against me. A guy poked at me, breathing down my back, about to shoot off, the chicks juicing up, hip-swinging into me. They came at me with high fives when I turned and showed them the power finger.

There was a crowd up ahead, wavering figures, at a pedestrian walk lit by low lamplight. A bright spot in the slummy downtown. We got there through one of those smelly alleys where bums pissed and jerk-offs drew "suck me"s and assholes. But, where the walls caught the lamplight, there were names and dates, scrawled or carved and spray-painted, some with glow paint. We came out on the walk, in a kind of moony light with snowflakes. I made out arches, dim shops, urns with plants, a flowerbed in a grill that was a chain wreath. The people shuffled along, all padded and muffled up, in stuffed jackets stiff as mattresses. Ordinary people, from businesses and offices, not trailer trash. With a whispery sound, as if they were walking on sawdust, they moved along a wall that led to a marble memorial, like the Rock of Ages at the cemetery. On the wall and the rock they wrote names, drew faces, did rubbings, with chalk and bright crayons. I saw somebody drip wax from a melting candle, it also had a shine. They brought flowers, left pictures, messages, luminary service lanterns. In the light snow, like skin flaking off, they dragged themselves by, falling on their knees, or lip-reading a name, tracing it with a finger that left a bright streak. Some huddled on benches like bums, just gazing out into the glow.

I used to meet Gemma in this place when I couldn't go home. She'd bring me messages and money from Mom. She had hooker friends in the alleys. One wore a fur, even in summer. She said she was walking it, like a dog. Close-by there was a strip joint that had become an overnight bar for people drifting by from the wall, mixed with street people, kids too, dropouts, like me in my alley cat days. A Good Heart sister helped out. She'd once been a topless dancer. The sign on the door was a heart. It used to be boobs but they'd turned it upside down. A singer sang a war song, Mom knew it. It was about women rescuing the souls of the dead from battle. In another skin bar the strippers were men. They came in the back way from Vic's Gym. I thought I saw one of them in a spot of light under an arch, I'd felt a draft go by, but it was a barebreasted statue, some sort of beauty goddess or fountain lady. The gang was still crowding me, I had to keep kicking them back. Some people had left, others came and made their glow. The voices droning on, fading in the silent snowfall, then loud as an echo over an amplifier. The tower clock gave long gongs, spreading gloom and doom. It sounded like a rock concert somewhere. And it picked up other sounds, I could hear breaths, heartbeats. You could see the breaths. In a while everyone began to frost over, in puffs of icy wind that left cracks in the air. Wrapped in their fleece-lined jackets, clinging to each other, they stayed on. Dropping down wherever they were, some had brought sleeping bags or silvery space blankets, a bum from the Sigmar Hotel sold body bags. The gang piled up on me, moaning and carrying on. Some shithead was all over me, trying to feel me up. I gave them the slip, cut through a catwalk to a loading area, where I hopped an Early Bird delivery truck out of town, the crowd still droning and glowing behind me, a gritty snow lighting up ahead.

17

I hadn't seen Dad's name on any wall, so I went out to the Barn to ask, as soon as the snow cleared for a day. On my "racer" with goat horns, the new handlebar Chad had fitted on it, with a rear-view mirror. And they let me right in, as if I was one of those gifted kids. I rang a bell that set off jangling chimes. Old Willis Ames opened the spring door. He used to be in the wholesale business with Dad, they shared office space and a phone in back of a warehouse, now he was in assisted living, bussed around with other oldtimers to the big box mall or his animal house meets. Shaky, in a tailcoat and a top hat, and getting emotional, he hugged and clasped me. Other old guys, too, gave me a squeeze or patted me on the head, they all knew me, I'd been there once with Dad, who'd introduced me, in his grand way: "This is Buddy, she's my girl". And I'd seen them in their shops and at ox roasts and benefits. Veterans of different wars, still keeping faith. Mostly in their Golden Years. They believed in that. And do-gooders, some days the Barn was like a community center. They ran a job fair, food baskets. They had praise and worship, under a spire, an Easter flower sale, dances, gun shows, potlucks, a cancer fund drive with pink armbands, outreach programs to get kids involved. Mom went for flu shots. Gemma held rehab sessions. The print shop owner was there, in Elder Care but still bringing out "The Merchant", where we advertised our hair parlor. So I was "family". Like Becky, who'd suddenly run up and jump into someone's arms calling him Papa.

We went in under the span of a spreadeagle. They were having their recollection, which was a spiritualist thing, calling up absent brothers in arms. Soldierly, at attention, chests high and heaving. A Founding Father watched from a column. He looked like Uncle Sam in the poster saying: "I Want You". A low gas flame in an urn burned under him. There was another kid next to me, Billy Buck from Buckstown. His dad had been in the Legion. A ballsy little guy with a crew cut, wouldn't talk to girls, just stared and went: "Shove it". I stared back: "Up yours". Puffed up and proud of himself but hanging on to my arm. Shreds of black sheets slapped around like flaps in a carwash. A guy rocking on his heels invoked Truth, Honor, Sacrifice. It was their warrior code. We swore an oath that was like a blood donor ad: "Make a fist!" Even pint-size guys standing tall. All of them in tails and Uncle Sam hats. A ceiling fan whirled, giving out streaks of light. It had a glow and was shaped like a star, with thirty two points, I counted them. At another speed the blades became petals and formed a rose, and we gathered round a shadowbox, which was a kind of jewel case with a display of medals on cushions, stars, crossed swords, a war cross, like one Dad wore on a chain, and a purple heart. Another box, with flying wings on the lid, held ashes, and in a glass case there were the sorts of relics Dad collected, brass buttons, cartridges and other trinkets, half the time you couldn't make out what they were, chips of bones, maybe fingers, dog tags, a locket that looked like a small shrunken head with stringy hair.

We stood draped in flags, between life-size cutouts of people they set up for the absent, some like the human-shaped targets they used in the shooting range, others where the shape of the person was a hole in the cardboard. Misty-eyed old guys who wore their medals like party favors, dangling rings, globes, anchors on key chains. It got rainy because some of the ceiling panels leaked, and we kept moving sideways. There was a rollcall with a drumbeat. We sang "Yesteryears". Call-ins came in over the speaker system. A scanner caught radio frequencies. A bugler played taps. It sounded like sobs and burps. Everyone doubling up, sort of coming apart, as if on broken hinges. I saw crutches and wheelchairs, a screwed-on head with a neck brace. There was one of those bionic guys who creaked and clicked like robots. Becky had told me about a dead man coming back in another man's body. Some of them seemed absent themselves, they nodded off and snored out loud, like old people falling asleep in the movies and waking up wasted. I smelled gas and noticed the low flame in the urn under Uncle Sam had gone out.

When it came back on, instead of Uncle Sam it lit up a hanging uniform called the Unknown Soldier. A ghost inside it seemed to breathe and blow ashes. Maybe someone who wasn't absent, just in hiding. I thought of my unknown dad. "Papa, are you there?" I stood firm with Bucky Boy, and they came and pinned tinny stars on us.

18

Then there were those waits in the trailers. With memorial candles, like wakes. Holly wreaths on the doors, heartthrob rock pounding. People plumped inside, hoping and coming down hard. Even the weather felt rundown. The air as if somebody had spit it out. A mess of rotten leaves, bare climbers like scars up walls. Mangy dogs wandered without owners. Guys were still coming back, from all over everywhere, but too late, a lot of them, even when they'd made it home, they went on wandering homeless. Some sad sack, supposed to be dead, but who turned up where he wasn't wanted anymore, got thrown out with his belongings. We heard the ruckus one night. And the bird cries of guys in nightmares. Parrot talk, another time. It was several sleepwalkers who'd met on a path and were shouting at each other. Dutch Early, Dean Eddie, Jackie Cobb, all fighters deafened by gun blasts or rock, their eardrums blown.

Guys with insomnia who couldn't sleep or wake up. There was a song about them, "Mystical Dreamers". By a Harley Davidson biker, Wolf Warren, who was a composer. One guy chopped firewood night and day. Once he'd chopped off a chicken's head and the chicken went on running around. Another guy had seizures. Suddenly he'd be jaywalking, he'd feel his brain sliding around in his head and lose his balance. Mom liked to talk to him, he said you could drop off the edge of the park, where kids went snowboarding, into a hellhole. There'd been break-ins and a hold-up at the minimart, and a Home Body, the Hobos, patrolled the grounds, taking over from the neighborhood watch. Mean guys, twisted out of shape, with stumps or bum legs, and night sights. And an old groundskeeper went around watering dead plants and feeding stray cats. He knew animal talk, like Becky, who spoke with skunks and coons, and he taught Mom an owl's cry with which nightwatchmen signaled each other.

Mom neighbored and sang when they asked her to. She had a thing going now. At parties or mournings, or just keeping somebody company. A lonely hearts song, at a candlelight vigil. In her hush hush style, she was perfecting it, a murmur behind almost closed lips, cool as running water. People bent in to listen. Or she'd let go, with Gemma and a keg. "Happy times" stuff, which always went over big. At a prayer meeting she sang "Man for all time, show me the way", they ate it up. Meantime she'd found a voice teacher downtown. A high-class guy, from a regular music school, cost her half our savings. For the technical side, just a few lessons, to get it right, he'd say things like: "Carry it in your throat but shape it in your mouth". She practiced good and bad breath and a dip down and back up through what she called the voice break. She showed it off at a yard sale, as something opera singers did, with Wolf Warren, the Harley biker, in a Hog jacket and Little Joe hat, making waves on an electric guitar. And then she did her singsong, which was what everyone was waiting for.

Work was going well, too, after a slump, when we'd been eating scraps, it picked up. Washes, tints, sprays, transformations, all with Mom's "vocals". Some ladies came just to hear her. Guys, too, shooting the breeze. Asking for a head, it was their big joke. She did an Elvis "duck", flattops, mullets, spikes and dreadlocks. Fitted a baldy with a rug made of plugs. A wrestler with a mop wanted highlights. He had shaved armpits. Another guy was a Baha'i, which sounded like Hawaii but was a world religion. He told me about a Babe they believed in. A nice guy, Arlan Elder, kind of dopey, a house painter, in hayseed overalls held up by suspenders, with rough hands with dirty nails and the look that he'd done a good day's work, came in to have his bushy beard trimmed and Mom let him stay on and fix our siding, which was peeling off. Others came for laughs. Bulletheads and high flyers with biker manes. Wolf Warren astride his bike, called Road Rage. They made her sing "Skyriders" and "Chase the Wind". Watched her rip into the songs, sometimes got inspired themselves and harmonized. A guy brought his spooky-eyed kid. I'd heard about him, they said he'd gone strange after they gave him his baby shots. Wouldn't look at you or speak, just rocked and hummed to himself. But Mom hummed along with him. Got him to smile, with a Mohawk. She had the touch. At any kind of a get-together, flipping a whopperburger on a grill, she'd come up with a smoky tune, maybe a bit of "opry" mixed in, to wow them. Some guy took her up on a hillbilly string, or there was a keyboard handy, anybody could get it going. She'd catch a mood like an earache. People said she guessed their thoughts. Or she crooned at a guy who was coming on to her. Got him up when he was down, she said. She teamed up with Gemma at Rosie's, they did their pole dance routine, swinging around on stools at the bar. Spicing it up, they ended on guys' laps. Mom went for the one with silky long tresses down his shoulders, Gemma liked them ornery. They did a "hotline blues", which was a strip, with the moves, but all in the mind, like phone sex. This was at the Lucky Lady Tavern. Got the guys so heated up they needed protection. A shorty in elevator shoes offered Mom his card. Gemma said he was from the mob. And there was a new Five Star Motel with a piano bar, off the interstate, its champagne ad bubbling on a tall billboard. A trashy area where drifters hitched rides up the ramp. Puddles of slop in back but SUVs parked out front, and plush inside, with a torch singer and a dance floor where slow-motion dancers flickered in twitchy lights. We gussied up and went to hear Savanna, the "torch". A hostess sat us: a Dora Belle in a pantsuit. Soulsearching faces around us, nightbirds at dim tables. All in a kind of fish bowl, because there was an indoor pool breathing damp air through the ventilation system. Gemma in her barfly style, Mom the fleshy beauty, in a sheath with a gauzy shawl. Putting on airs when they ordered fancy drinks. They danced with each other and I cut in. A ballroom dancing type couple did wrap-around figures. Others danced alone. The "torch" was deep throat stuff and sighs. A mouthy blonde in gold scales all the way down to a fish tail. Mom could do it, easy, and during a break she slithered up and grabbed the mike off its cradle, and the spot came on automatically and, noticing some Waikiki men who were causing a disturbance in the audience, she sang "Mystical Dreamers", in a sultry whisper. Sort of left a smear on the mike. Her updo came undone. It went in deep, you could tell from the silence in the room, and the accompanist, hyped as a "classical" pianist, said it was an art song.

The next time we showed up they didn't let us in, but Mom kept thinking they'd call her back. It was a countrywide chain motel, just what she needed for her fame to spread, if she could get a contract, and we did notice more people coming for a beauty hair-do in the next few days.

19

Dad was gone, his truck nowhere around anymore. But then one day I saw him in the mall, dressed as Santa. I was cruising with some girls from around town. Hip-hopping along, showing off our select styles. Glamor pusses and boppers, giving guys the eye. Bursting out of our dead-weight jackets, which we dragged along. We wore cover girl make-up, Day-Glo, lip gloss, blush. A lot of hot stuff went on. Flashing by, we got looks, didn't mean we paid attention. A great place to be, anyway. We had piped-in heat and music. Round and round, like a carousel, chimes playing carols, jingle bells, real Christmassy spirit-of-the-season. We drifted by frosted windows, snowfalls, holy hollies, trees hung with twinkly ornaments like eardrops or icicles. Guys hustled us along the way. Dudes wearing rings and bracelets, dropdown trousers with leg folds gathered at their ankles. Punks and mall rats, rip-rapping and tripping on their own laces. Stopping by an army recruiting post: "See the world!" In and out of stores, stealing and trashing. Losers getting busted. The crowd moving on. Townsfolk and backcountry gawkers lumped in. In a storm of lights, junk jewelry, boomboxes. Lots of jumbo types, beanbag-shaped women shoppers on motorized scooters, guys, too, letting it all hang out, barely holding up their bulk, leaning on walkers. Some on life support, with airbags and tubes, IV lines. A store called Tinkerbell sold glitzy beauty stuff, headbands, clinky bangles and beads, plastic purses, what have you, all pukey pink, cheap thrills, for chump change. We stopped at the Nail Salon, which was also a tanning parlor, and at a place where they did piercings: lips, noses, ears, tongues and tits and anything else you wanted, in the backstore, it killed you just to think of it. There were showcases down the middle of the aisle, cell phones, baseball cards. Our images streamed along with us, modeling the clothes in shop windows, reflected in the glimmers of the wishing well fountain. A watchmaker in a glass booth wore a goggle lens, looked at us with a huge eye. In Heavenly Bodies they sold body stockings and the like. Things people could see you through. In Secrets kinky stuff for bad girls, flip-top bras and peekaboo panties, it made your skin crawl, like being naked suddenly in public or seeing yourself from behind in a three-way mirror: "Is that me?" There were sure to be those fitting rooms where they spied on you, like in the supermarket bathroom and in tanning beds and at airport security when you went through checkpoints. We tried on Lady Foot shoes, scents and spices at a

perfume counter: "Yeah, the real me!" A store sold big
lady styles, with a Young Miss line for those already
headed that way. They looked like Dora Belles. We
stretched to every size in a one-size-fits-all house.
Made some wise guys happy: "Yo, do that again!"
Cute sales clerks, nextdoor. Not that you noticed.
But it gave you a stab somewhere. A Bird House sold
birds, tweeters and warblers. Mom had been coming
to see those. Some were bred or caught at Waikiki,
where a guy set traps for them, in the trees out behind
his Traveler, feeders and mirrors that attracted them,
and taught them songs, with recordings. "Seniors"
were being bussed in, golden oldies on a gift shop
tour. They made straight for the Dairy Queen and a
double dip toothpaste yogurt and whip. There was
also a Pretzel Dog, an Asian and Cajun, a Taco Tex, a
Live Well store. And we were into Lifestyles, Street
Smarts, which were tie-dyes and screen prints, Lids
for goofy hats, Fashion Bugs, like us, Game Stops
to play slots and videos. Death rays zapped us at the
entrance to stores, cash registers rang and checkout
girls chirped: "Have a good day!" Salvation Army
minstrels with their kettle waited outside. Security
guards shadowed us. Oglers and wellwishers going
by. There were night light places like Sea World, a pet
shop in an underwater twilight, and a dark sports bar.
We went down a side aisle where people got mugged.
Closed stores with broken windows, a windy storage
area and unloading zone, through a gloomy back
entrance with bins and a dumpster. On the way back
I got separated. I knocked around for awhile, peed in
a sealed-off men's room, which had girls' names and
phone numbers on the walls, checked out the laser

eye surgery place and Dana's Dance Studio where Snow Whites were rehearsing the Christmas follies.

And there was Dad, on an island in the center of the mall. In a Santa costume, a Bigfoot Snowman, up on a reindeer sled, the North Pole Express, in cake icing frost and clouds of cotton snow, acting cheery: "Heigh ho!" He looked like he'd been galloping by and got trapped in webs of powdered glass. In spite of his disguise I recognized him by his choppy gestures, the big booster voice in the bushy bear skin, and his duffel bag, I was sure it was him. Out of work, moonlighting at odd jobs and being hearty ho! ho! A hairy elf on a merry ride: "Jump in! One and all!" He had his own set of joy bells, a carillon sound around him, playing carols. So busy he pretended not to see me. Or really didn't know or care who I was? Kids lined up to sit on his lap. Or he'd snatch one up as he went by: "Gotcha!" He kept them bobbing and bouncing, clutched at a kid who was a spastic, you could hear his bones snap as he tried to walk without help, kicking out his legs. There was a lumpy ballerina in tights and a tutu. Doing flatfoots and pointy toes. Ballsy kids tugging inside their pockets: "Get a load of this!" The next guy with his bulge sneering: "Big deal! You got one, too?" Dad bandy-legged up there, like when he swung his weight into the dump truck and blasted off at the speed of sound. On his trip to nowhere, as Mom said. A jolly, ruddy-faced Santa, straight from Central Casting, squat on his haunches, with a bristly beard, cheeks puffed up like bubblegum, keeping up a one-man show with jingly sled music, a magic pass, when a kid asked for something, as if he were pulling it out of his sleeve, while it snowed on him. Maybe it was volunteer work, the kind the animal house guys did, barn raising, delivering meals on wheels, Helping Hands. Or make-work stuff, one of those minimum wage keep-busy welfare programs. Cookie crumbles all over him, mixed with snowflakes. He'd been sharing munchies with the kids. One offered him a soda and he blew bubbles like blisters through the straw. They plucked at his beard and knob nose. He pretended to fight them: "Put up your dukes!" He had a growly paunch. Tilted his head, cupping his ear, when they made a wish: "How's that again?" Greeted and hugged them: "Howdy-do!" Crunched their bones: "Love ya to death!" like he used to say to me, or when he socked Mom on the back to unplug her lungs. He had watery eyes, smelled of booze and sweat. Overstuffed in his cushions and woolens and long socks and boots. A bit sooty, too, with all those sticky crumbs on him. Or maybe he was just down the chimney. Still in hiding, running from something, covering up with his bluff ho-ho-ho! Old blowhard Santa bearing his bag of gifts, like some happy hobo, or the Bagman, putting on a scary face. He told the kids he couldn't promise, he'd do his best. Took some requests over a toy phone line. Got a voice out of a shy kid, more or less projecting it into him, like a ventriloquist. All with that breathy smell. Sour as Gemma's worry breath. I could feel it yards away. And he squirmed, needed to go to the bathroom, but didn't dare, probably afraid he'd be sacked, he had to wait for his time off, every couple of hours. One reindeer's antlers came off and he tried them on and went into a top-heavy balancing act. Meantime he shifted uncomfortably in his pants. Looked like he had flops slopping around. And full of aches and pains. A great upheaval, when he finally took his break. Hoisting himself up off the seat, giving out his boozy smell, now pissy, too. I suddenly realized he was disabled, I wasn't sure in what way. Sick? Wounded? Or was it just his weight? Landing hard, his knees buckling, he made his way laboriously into the bathroom, around a bend in the corridor. He crashed through the door and stood straining at the piss bowl, trying to unzip. His body wrenched and twisted, working his lips. I tried to help him position himself, but he pushed me aside: "Thanks, Bud", which wasn't the same as if he'd said "Buddy", could mean anyone. Never recognized me, or pretended not to. He managed to get himself undone, stood there some more, going through his exertions, but nothing came, so he backed into a toilet and took a loud crap. Jampacked in the stall so he couldn't shut the door. It was half out before he got the overloaded Santa pants off, and when they dropped I saw he was wearing a diaper. He tore it off, wiped with half a roll of Ultra Plush, smothering the drainage system, hitched up and shambled back out to his Santa post, in his fake furs and muffs, a snow king on his throne, or a playing card king of hearts. Mom used to say he had a heart of gold. Kiddies were mobbing him. A rat-a-tat gang with machine guns, walking spacemen that beeped and flashed. He waved me away.

It was the same story when I went back the next day, in the county bus, which Tiny Tina was driving now, instead of the special-ed minibus, she let me on for free, at a stop with a nativity scene, pointed me to a row where there were two empty seats side by side, because she thought there was another person with me, a problem she had when she was tired and saw double. Dad, in his winter wonderland, looked tired, too, haggard, worn out by his long hours, nearly falling asleep, off his sled. I remembered his fear of what he might do in his sleep, out of control, run wild and kill, rape, anything. He shuffled around in his costume, played the grouch or growling bear with the kids. Some upset him with their requests. Instead of presents, they wanted a dead pet revived, a mom or dad back from the war. Flaky snow sprinkled him like dandruff. Or maybe he was brushing off tears. The jingly carillon music, on some sort of a roll, on and off, was malfunctioning, it started in the middle of a carol and stopped in the middle of another one, then played slower and deeper, as if winding down. A heating duct overhead blew hot air in, vents sucked it out. You couldn't breathe. Kids skipped and skated by. One did a flip on a skateboard. It grated on his nerves, already strung out, then something got him going and he began fuming and stamping and worked himself up into one of his rages. He swore at a security guard, hassled a cleaning woman who went by with brushes in a bin, sweeping up trash, a gypsy worker. Wheeling around in every direction, they were closing in on him, clear as day. He started bellowing: "Balls to you!", holding his junk, as if he was about to throw it at somebody. The kids ran away screaming. He staggered a couple of steps after them, then tried to straddle a fork lift in a farm machinery display, a claw on a crab leg. He bucked and butted with imaginary antlers, like a trapped stag rampaging.

Security guards and cops grabbed him. He lashed out
at them. In a real frenzy. They shot a stun gun at him,
two sizzling darts on wires. He went down pawing
the air, and dragging a foot as if it were on a chain
they hauled him off and away in a K-Nine cruiser,
said they were going to lock him up overnight, "for
his own protection". They'd patted him down through
his Santa clothes and found a handgun on him. I knew
one of the cops, Dwayne Drew, a shoot first kind of
guy, but a pal of Mom's off-duty, he used to live in
Waikiki, in a Coleman pop-out, and he let me ride
in front with him. Dad behind in the dog cage, still
sputtering but doped by the shot. Oozing his pissy
shitty smell. He got booked, behind a bulletproof
glass, had his mug shot taken. Watched himself in
a one-way mirror, one of those police station spy
windows. Bars and cell doors all around, guards with
jangling keys. Another sort of animal house. Like a
zoo dark house, creatures cringing in corners. Creeps,
lowlifes they brought in zip-tied. Bums and drunks
sleeping it off, some of them patriots who'd crashed.
A gaggle of noisy hookers behind us said hello.
Happy showgirls, picked up as they were, tricked out
in girdles, body stockings, fantasy wigs and big-cup
bras that said: "Support our troops". Mom had
"done" some of them. She liked their back-and-forth
talk, said it was their work song. They were claiming
to be social workers. One called Dad "Santa Baby".
She played kitty cute with him, said she had a wish
list. He doubled up and retched, but signed in with
a flourish. Suddenly breaking free, reaching out for
support, he clung to me, I couldn't get out from under
him: "Ease up, Dad!" Some Hollerers bustled by,

visiting, which was something they did. It was Doctor Joy and his Christmas choir with tinsely wings and halos, singing: "Happy Birthday, Jesus!" Dad not quite going to pieces. Shoved along, seesawing, he rumbled into a cell. They let me stay with him for awhile, sitting on the bunk bed. Not a Slumberland mattress! The girls in the next cell made farty, barfy sounds, rattled the bars. The Hollerers were still around, singing a spiritual of theirs, about a place called Jubilee where it was summer when we were in winter and day when we were night. We'd learned about opposite seasons and hemispheres in school, but no one believed it. Dad stinking up the place. Just being himself! Now he recognized me: "Hey, Buddy". I tugged at his Santa beard, which he was still wearing. It wouldn't come off, it was his own, he showed me, grown out and gone white. Affectionate, in his bumbling way, as we sat there, in a bear hug, he said we were an awesome twosome. Whispering low because the walls were bugged. We did our goodbye: "Poke-you-in-the-eye!" And he kissed me, first time ever. A gloppy buss all over my face. Said he'd been saving it for me. But then he started ranting and raving again. Lucky for him he was locked up, because that night some crazy guy in town beat his family to death, and it could have been him. A lone ranger who got away, dumped his TransAm and ran for cover in the bush. There was another manhunt, search parties, all the same guys joining in, firemen, patriots, whooping it up, a posse with sniffer dogs, trackers, hawkeyes, with all their equipment, goggles and telescopic sights, a skyhawk overhead signaling, flares like fireworks. They scoured the fields, beat the bushes, chased shadows, sounded an all-points alert, even an air-raid siren they were testing, but they never found him. And when I went to see Dad in jail the next day he was gone again, they'd let him loose or he'd broken out, in the commotion nobody knew.

20

We waited for him, all winter. Sure he'd bust in on us at any time. We imagined him knocking around the bars, getting into fights, guns blazing, as some guys had been doing, maybe blowing his head off in some suicide game, but they hadn't heard, at the Barn or the gun shop or the recruitment post at the mall where he'd been hanging out between shifts in his Santa costume.

It was the worst winter in years. Storms and blizzards and about fifty below with the windchill! Snow shoveled down on us, our skin chipped off the minute we stepped outside, layered and muffled. Kids with frostbite when the schoolbus got stuck in a drift and we had to walk. Everyone crippled or cracking up. A lot of those guys with war stress. Soldier's heart, Gemma said. She did her therapies on them, when they started "acting up", not just teaching them moves, much of it mental stuff, like thinking big, to give themselves a build-up, talk cures to get things out. Roughing them up a bit, "kicking ass", she got them back on their feet, but they bummed out again. Half of them on uppers or downers. All loaded up inside. Sweet-natured guys suddenly beating up on their families, drinking themselves out cold. Or stuffed into themselves, in their overheated rooms, they tossed and moaned and had sweating fits. One guy in a house up our lane set himself on fire. He said he was meeting his Maker. Poured kerosene on his head and lit a kitchen match to it. They hosed him down, rolled him in cinders. Frozen guys turned up, out of foxholes where they'd been hiding for months. Some were still out there, fighting or running for their lives. There was still a war raging somewhere, bodies coming in, though in a news blackout, the guys said, so nobody would know, it was a cover-up. We heard rumors, about the survivalists: that they'd been blasted out of their bunker by an assault team in monster armor. And about aliens poisoning wells and waterworks. Enemy combatants hiding out in the state park. Others gone underground, a bunch had been dug up by a snow plow. We'd known where to find them because of Huey, a lone buzzard crow still wheeling overhead, long past crow season. Becky was the first to sight him. She had a toy telescope made from a gun scope. And once when she got off the schoolbus at the wrong stop and wandered, she saw snow angels.

At home our heat broke down, we spent the night in a shelter. Lying there, hanging on to our things, we heard stories. A masked gunman had shot up a fast food joint that hired gypsy workers. He turned out to be a guy with half his face gone. There was a copter crash on Two Top. A break-out at the "correctional facility" in Little Acre. Diehards and deadenders who'd taken hostages. Barns had been catching fire, struck by lightning, or maybe it was arson, a bridge had collapsed or maybe a terrorist had blown himself up with it. Ambulances, fire trucks clanged by.

Then, in spring, we really saw it. The way people came out, fat with grief, like the preacher had said. Hauled themselves around, trying to get things done, on ham hocks, or sat on their haunches with their blobby babies. Brooding and gorged with sleep and guzzling beer. Thawing out in the garbage smoke and the stink and froth of the river. Some trailers never opened, empty or abandoned, used for storage or rusting away, waiting for a "scratch and dent" sale. So lopsided you could kick them over, except they might be booby-trapped. And not much to do, with jobs disappearing, gone overseas. Sort of a general slowdown, like heavy weather. A cloud of quarry dust up where we were. People belly-up in bed at night, worried, beating themselves like old mattresses in the morning to wake up. They rattled off in their junkers to look for work, or killed time all day watching ball games. War games, Mom said, live and reruns. Snoozing in some broken-down truck they were tearing up for parts. Like tired wrestlers when they quarreled. They sat on their porches eating out of paper bags, putting on weight, hard bodies gone soft as play dough. The missing, too, fat absences around them. Mountains of flesh that could barely move, they made earthquakes of effort just shifting their bones in place. On disability, food stamps, you saw them at the supermarket, heaped on bent crutches, walkers, in back braces. Lots of business for Gemma, she had them working out, doing pull-ups, hobbling along in single file like a chain gang. Some fell flat and couldn't get up. There'd been amputations, because of injuries or "sugar". And those bionic guys made of spare parts, "good as new". You heard their junky sound going by. Others with their heads pounding. Like a beat of hard rock inside them. All trying to make it back from wherever they were. There'd be a loud party. Guys rotating in and out. Doing their grinding movements till they were worn down. Or some guy with a burst of energy, divinity, Mom said, walking on his hands. Happy to be in his body, maybe just broken out of a cast. There were those nightwalkers, a guy with an oxygen tank strapped to him, like a deep sea diver, breathing through a tube, and an old stiff who pushed an IV line on a sort of clotheshorse on wheels. Airheads plugged into voices, music, some near-death experience. Earl, the Hawaiian, did his rounds with his hit men. Raking it in, evicting deadbeats and squatters. "Sweet Leilani" ululating over his loudspeaker. There were foreclosures, with the sheriff reading out the notice, people just handing themselves over, even the big guns, too far gone to put up a fight, selling their things in warehouse auctions and yard sales, busted bed frames and appliances, clothes, trinkets, "collectibles" set out on card tables or a door laid across two sawhorses. "In living memory" one banner said. Jack Bargain, the hard luck man, stopped by to take his pick. Looters made off with anything of value that was left out. They came from the railway shacks and rooming houses. A soup kitchen picked up tables and chairs. Some families left everything behind, others hunkered down, tried to borrow from the loan king. That was the "broker" with his smug mug: jowls and double chin and a combover, grandstanding at his desk, hogging space and air.

We'd been having power cuts, backed-up sewers. The Hollerers came around with their Faith Van. Out of the Salvation Ark, which broadcast locally, from a rickety transmission tower, music videos where the spirits of the blessed danced like those balloon clowns rippling in the wind at gas stations. Speechifyng and baptizing, not just in the river anymore but at the fountain in town, or running people through the carwash that turned itself on and off, and in Waikiki we had a fire hydrant. They ran a funeral home downtown, a mummy house, with dolled-up bodies, known as guests, in viewing rooms, kept fresh and scented by an embalmer, who was a kind of taxidermist, all waxed and powdered and touched up. I'd been there with Mom when she sang for somebody. The "guest rooms" had themes, represented in the wallpaper, with names like air fresheners, Ocean Breeze, Mountain Dew, Island Spring. Some smelled like soda pops, kiddie rooms. There were remembrance wreaths that said: "known but to God". A stretch limo, half a block long, parked at the door. For kids they used Joe Marvel and his white Cadillac. The "guests" raised on satin cushions in their caskets, foreheads bulging out like mounted heads. The ladies with showy hair-dos. Mom had styled many of them when they were alive. Gospel and soul floated in. Becky's mom had a ministry there, so did Doctor Holiday, who always winked at me. He brought mourners, known as the Crew. You couldn't see them, because they were black, Becky said, as if they were naked, hiding in their skins, but you heard their chants, and Mom would go in and do "woes" with them, if it was somebody she knew. A mortician called Yule stood by wringing his hands. He believed in the rapture, a force that pulled you out of yourself and into the light, up a chimney. When the bodies, which weighed a ton, let out a gas, it was their souls leaving them. You could weigh them right afterwards and tell the difference. Nothing left of them but their pancake make-up death masks. Sometimes you saw a ghost, but we weren't scared, Becky said ghosts were just skins without bones. She knew where they kept the bodies, called remains, before being stuffed and becoming guests: in cold storage, in slots, or on hooks, like cuts of meat in the slaughterhouse, hanging by their chins or scalps, their guts sticking out, dongs dripping icycles. After the viewing they were transported to the Longmeadow cemetery. Sometimes so bloated up that the casket split open in the car and they couldn't get it out. The tombs, with inscribed monuments and florals, were up grassy paths into havens, glens and dales. They had send-off prayers and a lesson, about the generations of man, which meant our ancestors, back to the beginning of time, who were still among us, the dead that outnumbered the living. The angel choir might sing something, or a gifted kid with a faraway voice. I sang once with Mom, "Take me home where I belong". I was good at hallelujahs. Becky said I sounded otherworldly.

There were tombs in the trailers, too. Silent homes like burial mounds, trash piled up behind, as if a twister had been through, people digging around for valuables, sometimes the family itself, with noplace to go after being evicted, broke in to spend the night. Turned to stone by morning, they couldn't be moved.

And some abandoned trailers, out by the landfill, had been taken over by the gypsy campers. Whole families moving in. Piled into a Nomad or a Caravan. Crop pickers and day laborers, factory workers, milkers at the Daisy Cow Dairy. Mom knew many of them and liked to speak to them, and they laughed at her accent. They had stores and a church in a shopping court. Cooked spiced-up food in hot sauce, it could burn you to a crisp, and grooved to brassy music. The women all pregnant, squatted wide-legged when they sat and fanned themselves with their skirts, hot as ovens. They did their laundry in the river, slapping the wash on the rocks, threw firecrackers on holidays. Big kids used little ones as toys, babies scratched around in the dust, runty dogs dragged their butts along the ground. Some kids came for me once when I was feeling left out. I'd seen them playing with bones they'd dug up in the dump. They looked like human bones: kneecaps, a jawbone, a cracked crock that was part of a skull, with eye sockets, they hooked it on a stick and set a crown on it, woven of a thick braid and tinsel, Mom would have been proud of the confection. Next, they brought out a little girl in a lacy white dress, a kind of doll bride, they brushed her woolly hair, tilted her back so she'd cry, held her up under the arms to make her pee, then sat her on some cement steps to nowhere, just up into the air, with her head in the skull, and lit a candle on top of it. They'd stuck stickers of arms and legs on her, gummy cutouts from a dress-up doll book. Their brassy music going in the background, a smoky shape rose from the flame, like a ghost or a snow angel. A kid who'd got the Word said: "Holly Holly". He wore a lei, which was a Hawaiian garland. Others plugged into their Walkmen. Bang Bang was running around, doing his shoot-out. The little girl in a sort of heat wave or halo, the kind the Hollerers called a glory. She had twiggy legs and arms. Sagging off her seat, she went limp, as if she'd fainted, the skull fell off, and they passed it around, each of them trying it on, and a kid in a bomber jacket chased me with it, a ratty mutt gnawing at my ankles. Numbers of them lived in junked cars down the slope. Their belongings scattered all around them, like Papi's family when they'd given everything away. Our guys shoved them around. I saw them goose one of the girls. A mission fellowship ministered to them. They said they had an Antichrist hanging upside down in their church. Mom loved that, and a midwife in a hut, an old witch, who was about a hundred years old but had blazing black hair down to her waist. She'd been seen crouching and leaving a wormy turd. A hen had laid an egg in it and hatched a snake. Another lady plucked chickens when they were still alive and knew how to wring their necks and leave their heads dangling inside the skin instead of chopping them off, so they wouldn't bleed. Sitting out on the porch with Mom we'd hear their celebrations, and they invited us to a "giving-away" party, where they asked Mom to sing.

A family that was being deported was handing over a newborn baby, which could stay. A patriot family was adopting it. Someone said the mother had made the baby for them. It was prettied up like a glittery saint. Uncles and aunts and grandparents, from both sides, everybody cried but was happy for the baby, and the brassy music started up, and Mom sang things I'd never heard before.

She was having some of those bad days when she saw shadows like dirt in the light. Life fading, just like that, people looked pale to her, whited out, like photo negatives. Wondering if she was alive sometimes, she had to blow on a mirror to see her breath. A nervous wreck when they asked her to sing, afraid she'd lost her voice. She was really low, for no reason. It just came over her, dragged me down, too. We'd feel the pull of the river. Like a slug or a nightcrawler down there, scum and slime, roiled in the dark, all the crap you heard it carried boiling up from the depths, shitty sewage, chemical waste, fertilizer run-off, whatever, you could taste it, seeping through you, churning in your throat. I'd been fishing and seen a frog with three legs, and an angler caught something that looked like an oversized oyster, but with long hair, swum in from somewhere else or flushed down a toilet. One day we walked along the edge of the water, smelling drainage and swampy rot from upstream. Bugs flitted in our faces, little winged specs of ash from a coal burner. Oldsters in shacks watched us from their back porches. They'd brought out rockers and lazy boys. One old cuss in a ripped-out car seat spat and missed-- a sharpshooter. Soapy suds went by in tangles of driftwood. The gypsy campers were hanging wet clothes on a wire fence. They looked like flapping pelts at the tannery. A long-legged bird waded out, ugly as an ostrich. Reeds floated by, probably with people underwater breathing through them. Going with the flow. A guy was panning for something, somebody else threw a net out. Mats of grass got stuck in whirls and eddies. And we were almost sure a waterlogged trunk with stubby branches that snagged for a moment was a body, we thought it might be Dad.

21

After that Mom was fine, back up to the surface, working hard, saving for our departure. Money in the bank and in her ottoman and shoe pockets. The weather was summery, outdoorsy, made the hair stand up on her arms, gave me weird freckles. School was out, I was ready, too. Getting it all together, practically on our way, just waiting for the call. "Sure as life", she told me, like she always did when I was in a hurry for something to happen: "It'll come". I'd been hoping, for a lot of things: "Some day". She took her singing lessons and practiced at Rosie's or wherever, any time they asked her. She even landed a gig once at the Valley Motel, which had adult shows. It was in the industrial belt, at the far end of the county bus route. They needed a fill-in for a belly dancer, just a one-night stand. Mom came on like a pro doing "Sweet Leilani", with hula hula movements and pretending to warble on the belly lady's snake flute. She didn't care if they made fun of her.

Across the road from the motel was the big city style International Shopping Court where several churches shared rented spaces. We'd go for the sights and sounds. Breast beaters and head bangers, kneeling barefoot on prayer mats and going down flat on their faces, you could walk over them. Fireball cooking smells mixed with incense. It was like another country. A stalled escalator would have led up toward a broken skylight. A storefront church used an old cash register with bells and pop-out flags as an altar. Its blinking neon sign said: "Give me your tired, your poor, your huddled masses". Nextdoor there was a Big Bucks Bingo with numbers on a lit board. And next to that a quickie mailgram service, "transfers, money orders". Then a liquor store with pinups, a wedding shop with window models of brides. Fittings were in a sweatshop in the back room. There were coin and jewelry exchanges, yoga and martial arts, a palm reader in a turban who was also a marriage broker. She sat in a cramped space behind a curtain like an election booth. We'd once been to a free clinic. They'd given us some magic herbs to breathe. At a "call center" with a row of phones we'd seen a woman wearing a cloak like a shroud. Deep inside its many folds, she made a wailing sound, just like Mom singing at the baby party. All the shops played songs, and Mom knew all the tunes, she picked things up out of the blue. The Twins said she had perfect pitch, meaning she always found a key note that got the others going, she didn't even know how, she just said: "It's out there". Though I'd seen her keeping in tune with the keyboard.

Meantime our place was falling to pieces, we owed the rent, our water and light were cut off half the time, but what the hell, people kept coming, sprawled on the porch as if it was a spa, having their hair and heads done. They brought eats and chitchat, facefuls of laughs. Munching and swinging back and forth, bitching about this and that, cracking jokes and networking. A sort of happy hour atmosphere, true confessions spilling out. Widows hooked up again, guys making babies right and left. Everyone on a binge or a diet or a lifestyle. Plenty for Mom to do. She hummed and crooned, spraying, highlighting. Then she'd be out "following the music". Wandering in the Waikliki night glow. Drawn out through our paper-thin walls. Suddenly caught in a flash of neon, she saw herself "in lights". Gemma said she had buzz. Sweaty bright, both of them, as if wrapped in Saran wrap, sooty sparkles falling on them from a fire that smoldered in the dump, bomber beetles bursting on the WAIKIKI sign and raining down, writhing on the ground, the coin wash with its whirl of sound blowing clouds of laundry softener out the exhaust fan. Mom breathed it all in, basked in the steamy hot days, which brought the guys out with their power tools, master builders and roofers. Everyone was doing upkeep and improvements, up at the crack of dawn, patching, weatherizing, even landscaping, planting border beds around mailboxes, adding a deck or a carport or a loft, "customizing", it caught on. The Hawaiian and his goons were renovating empty places, for sale or rent, new and "pre-owned", they sprayed homey scents, lit hearth lights, hung frilly curtains, potted plants from shepherds' hooks on the porch, and so on, held open houses with displays, like in a Modern Living magazine they kept in the office, you couldn't believe it when they showed a customer around "house and garden", calling the can the commode. Soon instead of Waikiki Park we were going to be Heritage Heights. They were preparing the new signboard. Planning ahead, with uncanny vision. Mom had sung at a housewarming. "By invitation only", how's that? We'd smelled baking cake. Though they served soggy chips and pink lemonade. But in a lantern-lit patio with a fake well. A Home Sweet Home doormat. A Keep the Home Fires Burning fireplace in the living room. Everything had a name. They gave out cards stamped The Management. There were new businesses, a health food place, a video shop, in a Holiday Rambler. Dora Belle now called herself an outlet. A souvenir shop sold Land-I-Love patchwork. The old crack house was a pay chapel. You dropped a coin into a "collection box" in the altar and reached an answering service. Gemma wanted to open a Body Works massage. Or she might be a home care consultant. And bigtime partying was back, with kegs and boomboxes, including people who'd left but kept returning, like tornado victims, camping out for a night in back of what had been their trailer, with friends and memories, singing their hearts out, celebrating disaster with a blowout.

We drove to the fair with Gemma. In a blaze of sound and light. Mom was looking good, me, too, after another growth spurt, Chad on our last ride had said I was a babe. I felt antsy and itchy in the heat.

124

We saw stunts and a puppet show, which was new. Two preachy farmboys with a jumping jack and a harmonica. The jack was called Yahoo, which they said meant Jehovah, which was Jesus. A carnival wheel spun. We bumped into Smiley the clown on stilts like candy sticks. There were geeky performers out of some sideshow, or maybe war casualties with freakish wounds. A skinhead had stuck hooks and safety pins in his scalp. A strongman swallowed ground glass and blew flames. In a fat man contest tubs of lard weighed in on a truck scale. Somebody held up a sign that said: "Right to life". War protesters collected signatures. Pacifists unfolded a peace quilt. They gave out hand flags at half staff. You could get them at the Nine Eleven Flag Shop. The organizers of the fair were one of the animal houses. They were raising money in the picnic shed, where we broke down and ate a box of mushy barbecued chicken wrapped in foil, with all the trimmings. That was in the evening. An oldtimer sporting a master mason hat was telling a crowd about animal houses in the sky. He said there was a goat house, a lion house, a bull house, a bear house, an eagle house and a ram house, you watched for them in the stars. A searchlight beam was turning up there.

We went back several times. Whenever we had a craving. We did all the junk food stands. The chiliburgers stand was there, with my pretty boy. Watching me, I could tell, from beneath his knit brows, with those deep eyes. As if we'd met before, like Mom said when she fell for some mystery man, that she must have known him before she was born. We were friends with the bandleader, up on the bandstand. He had Mom sing "opry", with wavering echoes. Lights flashed on her like slapdash splashes of paint. Pretty soon some guy was hanging from her arm: "Need a lift?" There was always somebody muscling in. Long-suffering joes, heart throbs or slobs with gory stories. Patriots who'd been gassed, burned or maimed, hunters shot in accidents. Those big shit guys of hers, chewing on a chaw or a beef stick. Some we met when they came to be styled. A wrestler on steroids called Vern wore a red wig. He'd been an army chaplain. He fought in a steel cage as Hank the Tank. There was Winston, the champion auctioneer, a big talker. He wore a signet ring with his face on the seal. I got along with them all, let them look at me. Like trophy heads mounted on the wall. Mom checked them out, kept them guessing, took one in for a day or two. I'd sleep out with neighbors who had a cot, or swing on the porch, while they wallowed in there with her. Some joker who'd seen his chance sidling up. Hadn't noticed until then what a big girl I was: "Got some for me?" Maybe a li'l smooch, hunh? Just kidding! Smack on the puss, like Dad.

Other times we sat alone on the edge of the porch. We lit a smelly tart burner. The night pulsing around us, the earth seemed to quake. The park in a sort of syrupy floodlight. Crickets chirped in the bushes, buzzing wings that made a big music, they must have had some kind of a sound system. Mom said they were master singers, they sang with their whole bodies. A sort of bug hymn. We listened for our long distance call, making plans. We had a plan we'd used before: buy a beat-up car for a couple hundred, drive it till it croaked, dump it and go on on foot and hitchhike. "That's how we came", Mom reminded me. Halfway across the country, she'd told me. I was supposed to remember all the way back to when I was a baby, practically. Once we'd driven for fifty miles on two flat tires. The only difference this time, she'd have to wear sunglasses to drive. She'd get me a matching pair, butterfly movie-star fashion shades, she'd seen them at the dollar store. Maybe we wouldn't even have to buy a car, Gemma or Mort Damon could drop us off across the state line. I'd see her dreaming about it as she spoke, gazing into space. Sometimes with her eyes closed, but they kept moving, as if following shifting figures. The place was a mess, clothes strewn everywhere, no way to sleep, since she'd get me up at any time to talk, nothing to eat, she was on a crash diet again, just veggies, carrots and burpless cucumbers. I scrounged around. We showered together in the outdoor shower, in tinny, rusty water. We didn't mind if anyone saw us. We walked around the house naked. Gemma said being in your bare skin was good for you. And better than naked was nude, which had to do with self-awareness, it meant your body was saying something, in body language. I liked the idea, maybe if somebody spied on me just then he'd remember me for the rest of his life. Mom said I still had my baby bloom, which lit up around me, adding to my honey coloring. I'd tried to show it to Jay Bard, who would have wanted to know, and he'd promised: "Next time, Angie!" So it could be any day. Mom so full of it it was like a panic attack. And I had my asthma. Up in our heights, breathing thin air, our heads spinning. Afraid the worst might happen, if

Dad came after us. Both of us panting and wheezing. I had to use my inhaler, Mom her respirator. We did "bellows" together. She made suction noises, like a plunger. Blowing on a rubber windbag Gemma gave her, she had one of her out-of-body experiences, which Gemma said were near-death experiences, floating up out of herself. The keyboard purred in its case like a cat. She'd been tuning with it. And at Rosie's she sang with Wolf Warren, the Harley biker, known as Highwayman, who'd written a road song for her.

22

By then she had a new guy. All atwitter over
him. A big lout with a problem: he didn't know
who he was or where he'd come from, not from
Waikiki anyway, didn't remember much of anything,
because of amnesia, he said, another war sickness.
Just a survivor. Out of the wild blue yonder, wearing
another man's clothes, he wandered by one day, as if
coming back, but to the wrong place. In a mailman
jacket and rolled-up trousers, roped at the waist, with
a dazed homeless look, and chuckling to himself.
A bearish guy with a big load of body on him, I'd
seen him ringing doorbells, asking questions, like an
out-of-town census taker who'd been run off the park
recently, he seemed to get a laugh out of having doors
slammed on him. I followed him down to the river,
found him on his knees, splashing water in his face in
handfuls, sort of drinking up his image as it floated to
the surface. Hunched over under his heavy shoulders,

I almost thought he was Dad, from behind. "Yeah?" He seemed to have heard my thoughts. He turned a thick neck to glare at me. Then gathered himself and followed me up the slope. A shortcut I took him on, with stepping stones through back lots, a jigsaw path. Clambering, on all fours when he lost his footing. He caught sight of Mom in a shift, hanging out the laundry: "Hiya, lady!" And dropped in the next day with a posy, a bunch of wildflowers, as if he'd slept in a field. He wouldn't talk about himself. "Reckon it don't matter much". He joked about being a secret agent. He pronounced it "sacred". He said he was just passing through. Right down Mom's line. Like in her song "Gentle Stranger". He called himself Sonny, because he must have once had a mom and dad, right? He acted lost around the house and yard, like one of those tornado victims searching for memories in the ruins, or lounging on the couch, where there was a sinkhole, but then he'd whistle, two notes at a time, a trick he had, through two gaps in his teeth, and listen, as if he was on to something. Mom sang to him when he started rambling, in her hush hush style. Gazing deep into his eyes. Like when I did a close-up with Frisbee: "I like you just the way you are". She drank from a mug with him on the porch swing. At sundown, cooking a couple of burgers on the grill, which she'd never done with me. She said he was in a place where he couldn't get out, but she'd get in. Once he met me at the door with his arms crossed. "Going somewhere?" Laughing his little grim laugh. Mom was holding on to him. She had fingermarks on her wrist and a smudge of a smile. A while earlier he'd scooped her over the doorstep into the house like a bride. Somebody told us he'd been a prisoner of war. Gemma said he was "mental". Maybe one of those dead and born again. More like some wild backwoodsman, I thought. Becky had seen one shed his skin and another one come and put it on. He heard sounds no one else did. Like an invisible buzz high in the sky. He knew it was a drone. Mom convinced he was some kind of messenger or seer. He strummed heart music at her on an imaginary angel harp. He'd disappear for a few days and come back with another bunch of wildflowers that looked like a feather duster. And he had a thing for me. He'd whistle for me like I was a pet: "Here, Angie". Once he called me Baby Brownie. I was on the porch steps mugging with Frisbee, practicing a kiss, "quick and dirty". He whistled and asked: "Ever hear of a black Barbie?" I hadn't forgotten about the little girl in school who talked blank talk. She'd been carried in one day limp as a rag. They said someone had laid hands on her.

Then one evening he turned up in a car, an old rust trap with a sawed-off roof, a gun in the back seat rack, said he wanted to show me something he'd remembered from before, a place where he used to go. He'd shaved his head and wore a skullcap. The car hot-wired because he didn't have a key to the ignition. The steering wheel on the wrong side, like the rural delivery mail car. Empty cans scattered about like spent shells. A bumper sticker said: "Honk if it's over". I had to clamber in over my door, which was held with a rope. It was getting dark, Mom was in town auditioning for a talent quest agency where for a few bucks you could cut a demo track at a recording studio, it might be her break. We drove way out, along overgrown hedgerows, wind deflectors swinging on wires overhead, to where a fence rail sank and let us through, and we were in Camp Liberty, pushing up rutted trails, past Split Rock, into the foothills. Roaring and blasting out a double-barreled tailpipe. He was silent, hard-set and tight-jawed, biting down on his smile. He got out where we stuck in a rut and trudged on, dragging me along with him. He lit ahead with a high-power flashlight. I felt my skin bristle. When I pulled back he said: "Now, don't you try nothing". The car motor stayed on, backfiring through a broken muffler, but in a while we left it behind. We came to a glade deep in the trees. A watery moon overhead. Clouds like birds flying across it. I recognized the spot, as if I'd been there before, from a photo I'd seen in the newspaper. The census taker had been found there hanging by his feet, like the Antichrist, tied in duct tape. The shadowy trees leaned out in a faint glow. Nailed to one of them was a lone-wolf hunter's stand, on short legs, three feet off the ground. It showed up in our beam of light. We climbed up climbing pegs, through a plank door. Shifted in our clothes and bodies to make space for the two of us. We crouched there for maybe an hour, peering through a flap window. He heaved and weighed on me from behind. Breathed so hard that I breathed with him. I thought he was going to kill me. Maybe I was already dead. I heard his two-tone whistle, or just felt it, a breeze in my ear. It was a call. I could barely see in the moonlight, but I sensed something moving out there. It smelled of damp hay, a heap of dung. A shape appeared, a head of some sort, swaying and butting up against us until it poked through the flap window. A huge wet muzzle, a deer or a llama or maybe a giraffe, up high where we were! I couldn't see, but I felt its musky breath, and we petted it. Sonny whistled and whispered to it. I heard its lips working. It must have been eating something out of his hand. He held it that way for a moment before it drew back. He hadn't brought his gun from the car. He had a hunting knife in his belt, but he didn't take it out. "Our sacred?" he said, and light as moonwalkers we let ourselves down the tree and found our way back through he woods to the car, which was still running and came unstuck with a roar and got us home.

But the next day, on the porch with Mom, he was lost again, or wrestling with memories or whatever was eating at him. Really in bad shape. Shuddering as if he was about to have some massive breakdown, a stroke or a heart attack. He played with his 12-gauge shotgun, leaned on it, the barrel between his eyes. Banged the butt on the floor. Mom humming to him, under her breath, like when they were romancing. The next moment he stuck the barrel in his mouth. In his joking way, as if amused and wondering at himself. Rocking the swing gently. She went on humming: it was her singsong. She seemed to be going places in her mind. She had that hollowed-out look. Maybe imagining herself in some sort of spectacular music video. I remembered when she'd been expecting a baby a while back. Into her eighth month before something went wrong. She kept saying she was near her time. She'd done well at the audition, the celebrity agent, her angel, had told her she had star power, and she was dreaming. I could tell because she'd closed her eyes but they were still moving.

23

Then one day, riding my racer down the old mill pike, which used to be a rail line, a car ran me off the road. It wasn't Sonny, who'd disappeared again, lost his way or forgot where he was, but a camper van. I'd heard it coming round a curve behind me, making a racket, sighted it in my wide-angle mirror, on a drunken zig-zag, all over the road, as if bouncing off walls, then headed straight for me, but I didn't get out of the way in time. It side-swiped me, got tangled in the bike, dragging it along under the wheels, rolled over in the ditch and cracked up against a tree, and a man was thrown out the door, into the middle of the road. He'd been waving like mad as he aimed for me, as if he knew me, but I didn't see his face, and I couldn't pick myself up right away, after I flew over the goat horns and landed on my head, and I wasn't wearing my crash helmet. In a minute the car sort of gasped and swallowed up all the air around it, like some depth charge going off, and blew flames out the windows. Fire trucks came hellbelling, ambulances with air-raid sirens, and the big guys, volunteer firemen and rescue teams from all over the county, were doing their stuff, pumping his chest, breathing down his throat, wiring him into their machines, hoisting him on a stretcher, with a fluid drip and an oxygen mask, while others doused the fire, and there was Mac Snack, who jumped through the flames, right off his pure stock muscle car, to reach the shape of another person trapped in the blaze, though it was just a spook or a soul going up in smoke, and a medic in scrubs with a beer gut lumbered over to patch me up, and by then the man was a goner, but they hauled him off to Summit Hospital, where they were still trying to revive him an hour later, when I got there with Mom. Hanging onto a man's life, whoever he was, all of them, doing their thing. Fighters and high-flyers, mystical dreamers, like in the song, crowded into the emergency room, with raw burns and those hot eyes. There was a blind minister wearing foam goggles. He seemed to be looking through the eyeholes of a skull. And a doctor who spoke some foreign language, you didn't understand a word, which got everyone riled up. They wouldn't let me near the body, but they called Mom in to identify him, because she'd been "neighboring" with the gypsy workers down the slope, where she had another mystery man, dark as sin but with an inner light, who might be the right one, she'd been telling me, because she felt she'd known him in some previous life.

While I stood there bloodied and bandaged, and Mom not paying any attention to me, someone in a Harley jacket clapped a hairy paw around my shoulders. It was Highwayman, who lived out in the hills, where he used to take me to visit bat caves, in the days when he wasn't just Mom's back-up, and we were still best friends, he tried out his songs on me, and waiting for Mom to come out we rode around on Road Rage, rearing up and shouting into the wind.